Maddy

S. L. Sumner

Published by S. L. Sumner, 2025.

MADDY
First edition, July 22, 2025
Copyright 2025 S. L. Sumner
ISBN: 979-8-9992866-3-5
Written by S. L. Sumner

For my sister

"We can't take any credit for our talents. It's how we use them that counts." – A Wrinkle in Time

Foreword

This book is written for anyone interested in this important topic. Its pages do not include graphic material, but it is about a type of abuse rarely discussed. Fortunately, topics like this are finally beginning to be brought out into the open. If you don't want to read about this topic, or, if you feel it is inappropriate, please find another book.

This material is for two groups. First, it is for those in similar situations. It was written to let them know that they are not alone and to say that there is a life beyond their present situation. Help is available and it can be overcome with therapy and support.

The second group includes all who remain unaware of the struggles that lie beneath the surface of otherwise normal-appearing lives. Perhaps reading this book will bring needed awareness to the issue as well as provide some of the behavioral clues that may point to the fact that there is a problem.

The cover of the book has a door opening into a dark room. If you read the book its meaning will be obvious. However, it has another meaning as well. Secrets thrive under the cover of darkness but even the smallest crack or opening will let in the light. Darkness cannot overcome even the smallest of light and so dark secrets will fade when light shines upon them. Seek the help of friends, family, professionals, and authorities. Do not give up until someone listens and hears you.

R. E. Sumner, M.D.

Chapter 1

Footsteps

MADDY WASN'T PAYING attention, but she wasn't daydreaming either. Her mind had melted away to a sort of vague fog where thoughts did not form. Her last complete notion was a pleasantly surprised awareness that her headache was fading. This was remarkable since they rarely lasted less than a full day.

She did not stay away long, however, and soon began the gradual return to herself. As she did, she became aware of an uncomfortable silence around her. She tuned back in to class to hear the mildly frustrated sound of Mr. Daniel's question, "Surely someone can tell me how our main character knows who's walking down the hall? Remember, it's very dark and she's been asleep." The class was silent. "No one?" Silence. "Not one person has any idea?" Still more silence. Maddy realized she knew the answer at once; it was easy! Rolling her eyes and slowly sticking an arm into the air Maddy decided to put an end to the torture.

"Yes, Maddy?" She could hear the hint of relief in his voice and she was pleased to see him smiling down at her. "By the sound of the footsteps, they'd be heavier than her mother's," she answered.

"Good! Well done," said Mr. Daniels who turned to see Michael's hand waving in front of him. "Yes, Michael?" he asked with a wary look. The class was paying attention now; Michael's questions often proved entertaining.

"But Mr. D, what if the mother was really, really fat and wearing heavy shoes and the father was just a skinny little shrimp?"

Maddy sighed audibly and interrupted, "Don't be ridiculous Michael, the parents are described earlier in the story and neither of them is fat!" Annoyance was evident in her tone. The twinkle went out of Michael's eyes and she regretted her intrusion into his fun almost immediately. In fact, she was confused by it; she knew Michael well enough to understand that he was only setting up for one of his ever-popular distractions. Why was she being so disagreeable? Mr. Daniels stepped in.

"Maddy is quite correct, of course, but let's just assume for a moment that Mrs. Smith is indeed – uh—a woman of size while her husband is a 98-pound weakling. Michael, knowing that, wouldn't you still be able to tell who was walking down the hallway sight unseen?"

"I guess so," replied Michael.

"What kind of clues would help you to identify the walker?" asked Mr. Daniels patiently.

"The sound of the steps, I guess," said Michael.

"We have already established that, what else can you add? Think about it Michael, put yourself in the place of our sleepy protagonist," encouraged Mr. Daniels running his hand through his sandy brown hair.

Michael was beginning to regret his original question; he had only been going for a laugh. Still, he knew he could answer if he could just think for a minute, but the harder he thought the more stuck he felt. Mr. Daniels slowly paced the aisle as he continued to wait. After what seemed like an eternity to Michael in the hot seat, but what was actually only a few moments he asked the class, "Anyone else have an idea?" Once again, Maddy slowly raised her hand. Mr. Daniels glanced around the room hopefully for a new volunteer before he finally called on her, "Yes, Maddy?"

"Well," she said slowly, careful to keep her voice neutral. She definitely didn't want to sound like a know-it-all after snapping at Michael. "You might be able to tell by the speed of the steps, my mom tends to walk a bit fast compared to my dad. Also, she often wears house slippers which kind of slap at the floor and my dad never wears those."

Mr. Daniels smiled, "Well, I can't blame him for that, I myself never wear an open backed shoe; it just isn't done!" Several students chuckled at this.

"Of course, the point to remember, class, is that writers can make their work more interesting by using all the senses. Try not to rely too heavily on just what your characters see." A moment later the bell rang and Maddy overheard Michael's plans to try on his mother's gold two-inch heels when he got home as he left the classroom. She knew he wouldn't hold a grudge but she thought she'd try to apologize at lunch anyway.

"Hang on a minute, Maddy," called Mr. Daniels. Maddy sighed as she let her book bag drop back into her seat. She had hoped to make a quick exit.

After the classroom had emptied Mr. Daniels asked Maddy to take a seat near his desk. She watched his long, thin arms move quickly about the desk marveling at how he could easily reach from corner to corner of the spacious desk without even leaning forward in his chair. She waited while he searched around the many piles of papers wondering what he could be looking for and wishing he'd just get it over with. She was expecting a mild lecture about the way she had interrupted Michael.

"Ah, here it is. Maddy, I want you to take this home tonight and talk it over with your parents. I'm hoping you can take part in a young writer's conference. It's a two-day event that takes place in Orlando early in November. I forget the actual dates. Our school gets to send two students and I thought you would make an excellent representative for Chase Middle School. I recommended you to the principal and she agreed. What do you think?"

Maddy stared at the packet that now rested on her lap. "Uh, well, I – I don't think I'll be able to go," she said glumly. If Mr. Daniels was surprised by her response he did not show it.

"Do you think it might help if I called your folks?" he asked, adding, "This is really a terrific opportunity for you."

"I know," said Maddy, "and thank you so much, but I'm pretty sure I won't be able to go." She rose and heaved her book bag over her shoulder placing the envelope back on Mr. Daniel's desk.

"Well, take it with you anyway and if they say no, that's okay. At least they should know that you've been invited to attend so they can be proud of you. Let me know as soon as you can, especially if I have to choose another student," Mr. Daniels insisted. He handed her the packet again as she headed for the door.

Maddy left the room and started out for the cafeteria. Mr. Daniels was her favorite teacher and she hated to disappoint him. She decided to stop at her locker to lighten her load. Since she brought her lunch from home she didn't worry about waiting through the long line in the cafeteria and would have plenty of time to grab a drink from the shorter line for beverages only. She also wanted to ditch the conference packet before somebody asked her about it.

In the lunchroom she sat at her usual table in the back away from the kitchen. Jessica and Michael were already there.

"What did Mr. Daniels want?" asked Jessica immediately as Maddy knew she would.

Deciding to pretend she hadn't heard she plopped her lunch on the table and asked, "So could everyone tell I was irritable in class today?"

"I could!" replied Michael speaking in spite of the roast beef on rye that was taking up a sizable amount of space in his mouth.

"I'm really sorry about that, Michael," said Maddy immediately, "I don't know what my problem was."

"It's okay," said Michael, "I wasn't too bothered."

Jessica didn't give up so easily. "So why did you have to stay behind, Maddy?" "No reason, he just wanted to ask me a question and I answered him that's all," she replied.

"What was the question?" asked Jessica.

Michael saved Maddy the effort of a reply, "If she really wanted to share with us you wouldn't have to ask her twice, Jessie."

"Well," said Jessica, "I'd tell you if it was me, even if I had been scolded for something."

Maddy smiled to herself; she knew Jessica well enough to know that sharing her troubles would be the first thing she would do if she were held back after class by a teacher for a "chat". She was quite sure that Jessica would share everything complete with dramatic pauses for effect in an effort to gain the maximum amount of sympathy. Maddy knew better: She knew that few people really cared, even if sometimes they pretended to. Maddy took her lumps without complaint and kept going forward. Of course there weren't too many "lumps" at school. She generally got good grades and was well liked by most students and all her teachers.

"He really didn't say much, Jessica; I knew I needed to apologize to Michael without him having to say anything at all." *There. That should do it. It satisfies Jessica and technically it isn't a lie.*

"I guess so;" replied Jessica, "so, what's in the packet, Michael?"

Chapter 2

The Cassie Factor

MADDY HAD A LOT TO think about on the walk home from school. It wasn't a long walk, only a few blocks through the tidy working-class neighborhood of small, neat houses with lawns consisting mostly of neatly mown crabgrass and weeds. She was pleased to be recommended for the writer's conference, but resigned to the fact that her father would never allow her go. Her mother would be proud, but even if she wanted Maddy to go, she would never challenge her father's decision. If Maddy hadn't discovered that Michael was also invited, she wouldn't have even tried very hard to convince him. It wasn't worth the upset. Thank goodness for Jessica who noticed everything and always wanted to know all the details. Michael had received his packet before class and was sure his parents would be delighted to have him participate. Going to the conference with Michael would be fun, but how could she get permission? She knew her father would be concerned about cost, but his main objection would be the overnights away from home. Maddy was never permitted to attend slumber parties or sleepovers and she was sure the conference would be no exception.

When she arrived home she decided not to say anything to her mother right away.

She wanted a chance to look at the packet before opening up the topic for discussion. She went straight to her room to plan her strategy.

The room she shared with her younger sister was tiny. It held two twin beds, a chest of drawers, a small desk with a single drawer and some tall metal shelves that held board games and her younger sister's toys. The pale pink walls needed repainting, but they matched the similarly faded bedspread and drapes. On top of each bed was an oversized teddy bear, one reddish brown and the other tan. Maddy had dubbed them Red and Ted when she and her sister had received them as gifts from a favorite aunt.

She sat on her bed, pushed Red to the side, and emptied the envelope onto the bedspread. There were five things inside. The first to catch her eye was a glossy brochure from the hotel with photos of happy, beautiful people lounging by the pool, enjoying fine dining and relaxing on comfortable beds in suites complete with balcony views and flat screen TVs. She immediately decided that her parents didn't need to see that: it reeked of "too expensive". The next item was a letter of congratulations from the principal. She put that one on top; her dad loved to brag about her academic achievements. The next was an application. It asked for name, address, phone, emergency numbers, and required the applicant to agree to a "Standard of Behavior Statement" by signing below it. No problem there.

The application also required a 500-word essay from the applicant on their reasons for applying. Hmmm, reason for applying ... wonder how "just to get out of the house overnight for once in my life" would go over with the judges. Or maybe, "because I found out that Michael is going"? Maddy smiled to herself. She decided to write her statement before talking to her mom; her initiative in writing it would serve as unspoken evidence of how badly she wanted to go. The next sheet was a one-page summary of all the nitty gritty information: who, what, where, when, and the all-important how much. She quickly glanced at the "how much" figure. Ouch! $225.00. She realized that it was an excellent bargain including room, transportation, meals, conference fees and materials, but it was definitely a deal-killer in her case. She sighed as she looked at the final item from the packet: a permission slip.

She quickly reorganized the papers when she heard the front door open and placed them under her school books. By the time her mom popped in to see her everything was out of sight.

"Hi Hon, how was school today?" she asked from the doorway.

"Fine," answered Maddy.

"Can you watch over Cassie for me while I run to the store? I won't be long."

"Sure," Maddy replied.

"Why can't I come, Mommy?" asked Cassie with a pout.

"Because I can go faster on my own," answered her mother as she swept from the room ending the conversation.

Cassie sat on Maddy's bed. She had a curious look on her face as if she hadn't quite decided how to respond to her mother's abrupt departure. Maddy watched her with interest. She always enjoyed her baby sister, even though she was hardly a baby anymore at age five. Cassie had entered her life only six days after her eighth birthday and unlike some of her friends at school who had younger siblings, she had never been jealous or resentful of her younger sister. She babysat when asked without complaint and made-up stories and games to entertain her without a second thought.

Cassie had deep brown eyes and beautiful thick auburn hair that Maddy loved to comb and braid. Maddy privately considered her "the pretty one" while assigning herself the role of smart, responsible and practical. She considered her own looks to be nothing worse than plain, the sort of person who could fade easily into the background. She was medium height and build with brown hair and eyes that were neither blue nor brown. She disliked her eyes for some reason; sometimes more green, other times more golden brown, they never seemed to look the same as if they couldn't even settle on a color. Her mother called them hazel, but Maddy privately disagreed. In the dictionary hazel was described as "yellowish brown" never green and always the same color.

At the moment Cassie was sitting on her own bed busily pulling things out of her backpack and spreading them out in front of her. Maddy glanced over and smiled. She was, at the moment, trying to make her bed every bit as paper strewn as Maddy's even though it was more in her nature to be tidy. "I have homework, too," she said proudly pulling out a worksheet, "I have to underline letter sounds."

"Okay, want a snack first?" asked Maddy.

"What kind of snack?" asked Cassie.

"I don't know let's go look," replied Maddy getting up.

Cassie followed her happily to the kitchen where they settled on milk and cookies. Maddy reached up on a high shelf for the cookies while Cassie got out two plastic cups and the milk. Maddy had a hard time getting down the cookies; they were almost too high even for her. Her mother liked to keep them out of reach of Cassie and her notorious sweet tooth. Meanwhile, Cassie had decided she could pour her own drink. Unfortunately, the nearly full gallon jug proved too much for her. The light weight plastic cup toppled over and soon milk was everywhere. Maddy quickly clambered down and righted the jug before more milk could spill out. She capped the bottle and wiped it off before returning it to the refrigerator.

"Mary Cassidy Schmidt!" Maddy said between clenched teeth, "What did you think you were doing?"

"I just wanted a drink," said Cassie sadly.

Maddy sighed and resigned her self to cleaning up as quickly as possible. "That was a full bottle and way too heavy for you! What were you thinking?"

"When I got it out it didn't seem so heavy, but it got heavier and heavier, and the cup tipped and—-" she broke off unhappily.

"It's okay, but you'll have to drink water now. I don't want to use up any more milk. Take your cookies and go do your worksheet."

When Maddy returned to her room she found Cassie working quietly. She noticed that Cassie's bed was now tidy, as usual. Maddy pulled out the packet once again. Then she got out a sheet of paper and began her essay on her reasons for wanting to attend the conference. It didn't take long; she thought she knew what they were looking for. Besides, she had already been recommended and approved by the principal so it was probably a formality. By the time her mother had returned from the store she had a good first draft ready.

The afternoon passed without mention of the conference. Maddy finished her homework, worked on her final draft and watched television. When her dad got home from work she helped her mother start dinner. There was an uncomfortable moment between the two sisters when they noticed their mother staring into the open refrigerator.

"Didn't I just buy that milk?" she asked.

"We had some for our snack this afternoon," said Maddy with a look at her younger sister, "and there was a little accident."

"I see," said their mother, "well, at least I'm not losing my mind." Maddy continued to watch her sister, encouraging her with her eyes. Finally, Cassie confessed concluding with the unhappy complaint: "She used all three of my names!"

"Why Sarah Madison Schmidt, did you use all three of Mary Cassidy's names on her?" her mother asked with a smile.

"Yep, and she deserved all three, didn't you Mary Cassidy?" said Maddy.

"That's only two!" objected Cassie.

"That's because you're much better now, soon you'll be back to just one name again," teased Maddy.

Her mother smiled and gave Cassie a hug, "I'm so glad you told me; that must have been hard for you, but it's always better to tell the truth, isn't it?" She winked at Maddy as a silent thank you for handling the situation well. Maddy almost decided to bring up the conference at this point. Her dad was dozing in front of the TV and her mom seemed to be in a good mood but she couldn't decide about the "Cassie factor". Would Cassie be helpful, adorably pleading on her behalf, or might she blurt something out to her father before Maddy was ready for it? In the end she decided it would be better to wait another day and ask during the following afternoon before her dad got home. She could even check with Michael to be sure he was really going and maybe even ask Mr. Daniels to call her parents after all. Besides, if she didn't ask yet she could still have hope, at least for one more day.

Chapter 3

Clucking and Crowing

MICHAEL'S MOTHER PICKED him up after school. He had an appointment with the orthodontist which he dreaded. He had worn braces for almost a year and it seemed like they hurt worse after every appointment. His experience in Mr. Daniel's class also bothered him more than he liked to admit, even though it was nice that Maddy had apologized. He was more upset with himself for not being able to think on his feet and come up with an answer than angry at anyone else. *It wasn't as though it was a difficult question, only one that required some imagination; put yourself in the place of the character who woke up to hear someone walking down the hall. How hard is that? Describe the sound, stupid! It was the speed, fast or slow; and quality, hard soles or something softer.* It seemed so much easier now without Mr. Daniels and the entire class waiting on his answer.

Stopped at a traffic light his mother was looking at him with mild concern.

"How was school today, kiddo?" she asked, "You look a little distracted."

"It was okay, I guess. I missed a question in Mr. D's class," he said.

"Did you have a test?"

"What? No, it was during a discussion about a short story."

"Oh, so it doesn't count?"

As usual, she only cares if I've messed up a grade. "Mom, I'd rather miss a question on a test than screw up in front of the whole class."

"What was the question?"

"It doesn't matter; you haven't read the story anyway."

"I'm sorry Michael; did anyone else know the answer?"

"Just Maddy."

"So, you're upset that you couldn't answer a question that only *one* other student in the class could answer?"

"Mom."

"Maybe it was just an off day."

Okay, she's really trying now, time to get over it. "I guess so. Mr. D. also recommended me for some writer's thing in November. You can look at this stuff while I get my teeth tightened," he said waving the information packet.

His mother perked up noticeably. "That sounds interesting, who else is going?"

"I'm not sure. Mr. D said only two kids can go, but he didn't say who else they asked."

"Only two students have been invited! That's impressive, Michael! I can't wait to tell your dad tonight."

"It's no big deal."

"Of course it is; it's a very big deal to represent your school."

Now she getting carried away; probably shouldn't have mentioned it until after the orthodontist.

"Here we are," she announced cheerily.

Oh joy.

After his "teeth tightening" Michael was escorted back to the waiting room by the technician. She had her arm around his shoulder as if he was being comforted by a "dear friend". Michael knew what was coming next: a lecture about good oral hygiene and a reminder that he might be sore for a day or two and could have a mild pain reliever if he needed it. It irked him that this always happened in the waiting room in front of other people. They had this ridiculous rule about patients only in the exam rooms; parents were required to remain in the waiting area. That meant that follow-up instructions, kudos and criticism, were handed out in full view of others waiting.

"Michael did well today Mrs. Evans," smiled the young woman brightly, "He may have some discomfort for a day or so and you can give him some Tylenol if he feels he needs something." Here she paused and rearranged her face into a pouting frown. "We are beginning to be concerned about Michael's oral care. As you can see, if you look, his gums are a bit puffy and they bled a little while we adjusted his braces. These are signs of poor cleaning and can lead to more serious conditions. Proper brushing and especially flossing are so very important with braces and I'm not sure Michael is giving us his best effort." Another pause while she assumed a new expression of renewed determination. "With your encouragement I'm sure Michael will do better next time. We need to see you again in six weeks."

"Thank you, Sherri, we'll do our best to urge Michael to do better. Of course I can't brush *for* him," she added somewhat defensively. She turned her attention to the receptionist who was looking on sympathetically.

"Mrs. Evans I can get you in on November 21st."

"Oh dear, I'm not sure, when is your conference, Michael? Michael is taking part in a writer's conference in November. He was one of only two students chosen to represent his whole school!"

she smiled and paged through the information packet as though looking for the dates.

Yep, definitely should've waited until after the orthodontist.

"Michael, when is the conference, dear?"

"I don't know; you have the packet." Michael was sure his mother knew the exact dates of the conference by now. He had been with the orthodontist for 30 minutes and that was plenty of time for his mother to have read the entire packet thoroughly.

"That's not very helpful, dear," she said absently, "Oh, here it is," she announced triumphantly, "Yes the 21st is just fine; he'll be home by then."

The receptionist indicated her approval of Michael's accomplishment and handed his mother a reminder card for his next appointment.

On the way home in the car Michael's mother alternated between clucking over how embarrassing it was to be reminded yet again about Michael's poor brushing habits and crowing over his latest academic conquest. Although he was sure that his mother really did care about his teeth, he did note that the thrust of her complaints centered around how his bad hygiene reflected poorly on *her*. In the end he supposed it was good that the conference information had arrived on the same day as his orthodontist visit. That way she could split the difference: sometimes you get to bask in reflected glory and sometimes you have to wear sunscreen to shield yourselves from the harmful rays of burning criticism.

Chapter 4

Pulitzers and Permission

MADDIE ARRIVED AT SCHOOL early and headed for Mr. Daniel's room. She started to go in when she heard voices and decided to wait in the hall.

"We are very excited about the conference and I'd like to offer to drive and act as a chaperone as well."

"That's very kind of you, Mrs. Evans, but the school district is chartering a bus to send all the student representatives together. They will be chaperoned by nine Language Arts teachers from various schools who have attended a seminar on mentoring writing skills."

"I see, well, what if I just provided my own transportation and accommodations and went along as an observer? I like to be involved in my son's extracurricular activities as much as possible and I am fortunate enough to be able to do so most of the time."

"That's very admirable, but I think in this case it's sort of like going away to camp. The facilitators want the participants to be able to immerse themselves in the writing process without distractions during the sessions. They will take part in brain storming sessions to decide on their topics and hear presentations from local area writers. It is hoped that they will not only enjoy the creative process, but also pick up writing mechanics as they complete their final drafts. All of the student's work will be compiled into a professionally produced magazine which they should receive a few weeks after the conference. A few students will have their work published by the local paper. It really is quite an extraordinary opportunity."

"Well, you don't need to sell me on the value of the conference," replied Mrs. Evans, "I am sure Michael would be able to focus on his writing without being distracted by my presence. Am I to understand that no parents will be permitted to attend?"

"I'm afraid so," answered Mr. Daniels.

"Well, thank you for thinking of Michael; I know he will enjoy the conference."

"He's a great kid; I really enjoy having him in class."

Mrs. Evans beamed, "Please let me know if there is anything I can do to help."

Maddy entered as Mrs. Evans left.

"Good morning, Maddy, what brings you here so early?" asked Mr. Daniels, "Did you talk to your parents about the conference?"

"Not yet," she admitted, "I was hoping that you might call them after all."

"Sure, I'd be happy to. When is a good time to catch them at home?"

"My dad gets home around 6:30."

"How about after 7:30 to give him time for dinner?"

"Okay."

"Maddy, may I ask a personal question?"

"I guess so."

"Is the registration fee a problem for your folks? If it is we might be able to work out a solution, a sort of scholarship maybe."

"That might help, but I'm still not sure they'll let me go."

"Why not?"

"Well, it is expensive and also the overnight and it's out of town."

"I see. Would you like to go if you had their permission?"

"Yes, sir, and I know you need time to ask someone else, so I promise to find out tonight for sure."

"That's alright, there's still plenty of time to find an alternate, but maybe I won't need to," he smiled.

Maddy smiled too. She knew better than to get her hopes up, but she couldn't help herself. "I'll see you fourth period."

"I look forward to it!" called Mr. Daniels cheerfully.

Maddy met Michael waiting in the hall. She could tell he had been listening in.

"So, you're the 'other student,'" he said raising his eyebrows.

"Yeah, but don't tell Jessica, in case my parents won't let me go. She drove me nuts when I couldn't go to Melissa's slumber party last week. She just couldn't understand why they wouldn't let me."

"I don't really understand it either," offered Michael, "what is their problem?" "I don't know," said Maddy.

"Well, at least they don't want to go *with* you! Thank God Mr. Daniels didn't cave in on that one!"

Maddy smiled, "Yeah, what is her problem?"

"We all have our crosses to bear," said Michael melodramatically, "It would be great if you could go, though; are you going to ask them today?"

"I have to since I asked Mr. Daniels to call them tonight."

"Think it'll help?"

"Honestly, no, but I'll never know if I don't ask. I'm thinking that since it's school related and kind of a big deal to be invited maybe..." she trailed off.

"Oh, it's a very big deal, just ask my mom. She went on and on last night about what an honor and responsibility it is to 'represent one's school'. I'm sure she imagines me accepting the Pulitzer Prize for Literature at the end of the conference. I'm already working on my acceptance speech thanking all the little people and especially my sainted mother."

Maddy chuckled and shook her head. Michael could always make her smile. She wished she could make her problems with her parents into a funny story, but her situation did not lend itself so easily to comedy. "I just hope I can be there when you win that award."

"I'll keep my fingers crossed," said Michael and turned off down the hall to his first period class.

Chapter 5

Dad Sense

MADDIE RACED HOME FROM school, if she hurried she would have just enough time to finish copying her final draft of the essay before her mom and Cassie got home. She was rereading the final copy when she heard them arrive. She was surprised to feel her heart beating faster than usual.

They were in a good mood, singing a silly song at the top of their voices:

Oh, her head is as round as a pumpkin,

And she doesn't have one bit of hair,

So she wears an old mop and she calls it a wig,

There's none that my love can compare to!

What shall I do, what shall I do?

Enchanting Sophia I'm mad about you!

Maddy joined in on the last verse. She knew the song from her days in Miss Stewart's music class. It was one of her favorites. She was relieved to notice that her nervousness was gone.

She gave her mom a few minutes to settle in before bringing out the information packet.

"What have you got there?" she asked.

"It's some stuff about a writing conference. Mr. Daniels recommended me and Michael Evans for it. I already told him I probably can't go, but he's still going to call tonight about it." She felt slightly uncomfortable about making it sound as though Mr. Daniels had insisted on calling himself, but she knew she needed all the help she could get.

Her mom removed the contents from the envelope and began sifting through them. After a few minutes she looked up, "You'd really like to go, huh?"

"Yes," she said looking at the floor.

"It looks really cool; we'll have to ask your father."

"Your father"; that was a bad sign. She didn't say "Dad" like it was his name, like asking good ole Dad, but "your father", which seemed less personal and more like his formal position within the family. One must respect one's father and his decisions.

There was an uncomfortable moment broken by Cassie, "What's wrong?"

"Nothing's wrong!" replied her mother promptly, "Everything's good! I'm very proud of your big sister!"

"Yay Maddy!" sang out Cassie, "What did she do?"

"She got picked by her teacher to go to a writer's conference!" Maddy noted that her mom had begun speaking in exclamation points, trying to make up for her dad's inevitable refusal with enthusiasm for her accomplishment.

"It's an honor just to be nominated," she said dripping sarcasm.

Her mother sighed, "Honey $225.00 is a lot of money."

"I know," said Maddy inspecting the floor once again, "Well, I have a lot of homework." This was not true. She had two more math problems and four pages of social studies to read, she could finish both in half an hour. She went to her room and closed the door to pout a little.

Dinner passed without any mention of the conference. Maddy supposed her mom was waiting for Mr. Daniels' phone call. Maddy wasn't sure if that was a good idea or not. She didn't think her dad would like being caught off guard, but advance notice would give him time to plan excuses for refusing without looking bad to her teacher. Maybe if they caught him off guard he might say yes to Mr. Daniels. She was still mulling over possible outcomes when the phone rang. Both she and her mother jumped at the sound but her dad appeared not to notice as he picked up the phone. It was 7:30 exactly.

"Hello?"

"Yes, this is Mr. Schmidt."

"It's no bother."

A long pause while Mr. Daniels made his pitch.

"That's wonderful news," he was smiling, "Well, we'll let you know as soon as I have time to go over the information."

"Yes, she's a great kid, we're really proud of her."

"Yes, yes, I will. Thank you for calling. Good evening." He hung up.

"Well, usually a phone call from the teacher is cause for concern, but not at our house! Maddy why didn't you tell me about the conference at dinner? Mr. Daniels said you have an information packet to show me."

Maddy brought him the envelope. She had carefully arranged the contents earlier. Her mother stood in the doorway watching, "I told her to wait until after dinner. I didn't realize that Mr. Daniels would call and spoil the surprise."

Interesting. Mom is trying to help.

"He seemed as if he needed an answer as soon as possible, so he probably couldn't wait. Besides, I bet he doesn't get to call a parent with good news very often!" said her dad proudly.

"No, I guess not," agreed her mother, "too bad for all those other parents!"

Maddy and her mom did the dishes together. They talked about everything except the conference. Cassie helped too; her special job was to dry the silverware and put them away. She liked sorting them into their proper places in the plastic tray. While she worked she repeated, "and the dish ran away with the spoon," over and over.

Her mom watched Cassie and shook her head, "I wonder why she does that. Can you remember when she started?"

"She's always done it."

"But why doesn't she ever recite the whole rhyme? I'm sure she knows it."

"I guess because that's the only part that goes with doing the dishes, we don't have any cats or fiddles around here."

"That makes a certain amount of "Cassie sense"."

"What's Cassie sense?" piped Cassie at the mention of her name.

"Cassie sense is anything that makes sense to Cassie!" answered her mom.

They all giggled.

When the dishes were done Maddy helped Cassie with her bath. She decided not to watch TV and instead read a story with Cassie and sent her out to say goodnight on her own. After Cassie was all tucked in, she stayed in her room still pretending she had a lot of homework. The more time went by the more she knew her dad's decision. If it were going to be good news he'd have already told her. Just before bed she went out to the kitchen to ask her mom to sign a math test to be returned the next day, she had made a 94. Having it signed and returned was for extra credit; she didn't need the extra credit in math.

Maddy's father appeared in the doorway of the kitchen looking grim. He delivered his verdict and left without waiting for any cry of protest. He had made up his mind and there would be no argument. There was no use trying to reason with "Dad sense".

Chapter 6

Whisper-shouting

———◆———

MADDY WENT TO BED DISAPPOINTED but not terribly surprised. The official reason was cost and she had to admit it was an important factor, but she could hear her parents discussing it after she went to bed.

"I'll not allow her to go half way across the state and spend two nights in a hotel alone!" he insisted. He wasn't shouting, but if whispers could shout that's what it would sound like. She could hear him loud and clear.

"She wouldn't be alone, there are chaperones, dear," soothed her mother, "of course it is a lot of money."

Traitor! She's letting him off the hook!

"Two nights! With *strangers!*" he whisper-shouted.

"They are school teachers," she returned.

"School teachers who are strangers to us!" he hissed.

Much later her dad came to her room. He sat on the side of her bed and began to rub her back.

"I know you're disappointed honey," he began.

"I'm tired."

"Now, honey, I know you're upset..."

"NO!" Maddy whisper-shouted.

Chapter 7

Second Chance

MADDY HAD ALREADY ADJUSTED to her dad's decision; she just wanted to let Mr. Daniels know what had happened and forget the whole thing. On her way to his classroom she ran into Michael and his mother. *Poor Michael, does his mom follow him everywhere?*

"Hey Michael," she said.

"Hi Maddy, what's up?"

"Not much." Maddy hesitated. She correctly figured that Michael's mom was also headed for Mr. Daniels and she wasn't interested in an audience when she delivered her bad news.

"Maddy?" asked Michael's mom, "Is this the same Maddy who is going with you to the writer's conference? Why didn't you introduce me?"

"Mom, this is Maddy", said Michael formally with an apologetic glance at Maddy.

"How do you do, dear? Congratulations on being selected; aren't you excited?" she said shaking her hand.

"Yes, ma'am," she replied.

"Mom," interrupted Michael before his mom could continue her conversation, "Mr. Daniels is waiting for you."

"Oh, yes; it was certainly a pleasure to meet you, Maddy." She hurried off for her meeting with Mr. Daniels.

Michael knew the moment he saw Maddy that she was unhappy and he was almost certain he knew why. "So, I guess the news isn't good. I'm sorry Maddy; the conference won't be nearly as much fun without you."

"Thanks for getting your mother to go away. I didn't want to say anything to her because I haven't told Mr. Daniels yet." Maddy couldn't meet Michael's eyes, she felt as if she might cry if she did. She thought she had accepted this disappointment as she had so many others, but this one was harder somehow.

Michael was a little surprised by how disappointed *he* was feeling. Suddenly the conference was much less exciting; it might even be like work without Maddy to joke around with. He wondered who might be sent instead, probably a girl. They always seem to pick a boy and a girl for these things. After a moment Michael glanced at Maddy.

"I hope you won't be offended, but your parents are schmucks."

"My mom tried to help, but my dad wouldn't budge."

"Okay, your dad's a schmuck."

Maddy managed a small smile and to her horror one big tear came sliding down her cheek. She quickly brushed it away, but Michael had noticed.

They both turned to see Mr. Daniels and Mrs. Evans striding down the hall toward them smiling. Mr. Daniels asked Maddy to accompany him to his classroom and Mrs. Evans mercifully kept going down the hall with a small wave of farewell to Michael.

"Well, Maddy, I had a phone call from your dad this morning. He was lucky to catch me when I had a few moments to talk. He told me that the conference will be a little too expensive for your family and that you will not be able to go."

"Is that all he said?"

"Yes, should he have said anything more?"

"Just, just that he didn't want me away overnight."

"He only mentioned the cost."

"Oh." *No surprise there.*

Mr. Daniels was quiet for a moment, as though considering how to continue the conversation. Maddy waited, curious. She had expected to tell him she couldn't go and return the packet and be done with it.

"After I talked with him, I received news that money has been found to create a scholarship to cover expenses for both representatives to the conference. Do you think he might reconsider his decision?"

It was Maddy's turn to be quiet. Her dad had underestimated Mr. Daniels. He figured the school couldn't force a family to pay for an extracurricular activity so he only gave the "safe" excuse. He didn't count on Mr. Daniels' resourcefulness; she was sure he was behind the mystery scholarship. Not wanting to impose on his kindness toward a losing effort any more she decided to be honest.

"Probably not, but thank you so much for trying. It's really nice of you to go to so much trouble."

"Well, let's let him tell us that himself, Maddy, you might be surprised. Now it's time for you to head to class."

Maddy started off to first period her head swimming with a variety of thoughts and emotions. Exactly how had the scholarship come to be? Would her dad be angry at having to say "no" twice? Mr. Daniels was so nice. Michael was so sweet. She was afraid to hope but couldn't resist the impulse in spite of the distinct possibility of the disappointment to come.

Chapter 8

Breaking News

MADDY AND MICHAEL ARRIVED to find Mr. Daniel's fourth period class in an unusual state of confusion. The school news team was setting up to record an announcement from the principal to be made from their class. The principal, Mrs. Lunsford, and Mr. Daniels were conferring with the mass media teacher, Mr. Buchanan. A few of the boys were moving some of the desks to the perimeter of the room, while another pair set up a video camera in front of Mr. Daniel's desk. Jessica was in the center of it all going over her notes to introduce the segment.

"Wonder what's going on?" asked Maddy.

"I dunno," returned Michael, "my mother isn't here is she?"

Maddy smiled, "Oh Michael you think everything is about you! Don't you remember, the Pulitzer isn't being awarded until November."

Michael rolled his eyes, "Don't try to be funny Maddy, it doesn't suit you."

In the next moment, Maddy was surprised to see Mrs. Evans sweep in.

"Nothing gets by her," Michael muttered under his breath.

His mother hurried over, "Isn't this exciting!"

Michael shrugged, "I don't know; what's the big announcement?"

"You'll see soon enough," smiled his mom, "I don't want to spoil the surprise."

Maddy saw Mr. Daniels heading over to them. He spoke briefly with Mrs. Evans and asked Maddy and Michael to take the two seats next to Jessica near his desk. Mrs. Evans moved quietly to the back of the room while the rest of the students took seats in the circle of desks surrounding the room. Mrs. Lunsford was given a microphone and asked to sit at Mr. Daniel's desk for a sound check.

Mr. Buchanan addressed the class. He was dressed in his usual plaid shirt and jeans since he almost never appeared in front of a camera. He had instructions for the class.

"Good morning. As you can see, we are taping a short segment to be shown on tomorrow morning's show. It will only take a few minutes with everyone's cooperation. We will begin with Jessica who will introduce Mrs. Lunsford. Mrs. Lunsford will give a few prepared remarks and then make presentations to the selected students. Your part in all of this is to remain quiet, and I mean **quiet!** After both students have been announced you may applaud. Applause only! No cheering or hooting or whatever. Am I understood?"

Mr. Daniels stepped forward, "You can count on them to cooperate, Mr. Buchanan." He then turned toward the class with mock seriousness and said, "I know who you are."

The class tittered. Maddy looked at Michael knowing that this would be one of those times for a classic Michael comment, but Michael was still distracted by his mother's presence. She sat and waited, mildly curious to know why she was being included, but expecting that this was a lot of hoopla over nothing. Finally, they were ready to begin.

Mr. Buchanan cued Jessica – holding up three fingers, then two, then one pointed at her as her cue to begin.

Jessica, outgoing and confident looked into the camera and smiled. "Good morning! We are reporting from Mr. Daniels' fourth period Language Arts classroom today to announce the selections for this year's writer's conference to be held in Orlando. Since both representatives are in this class we decided to make the announcement in front of their classmates."

At the mention of their class a few students cheered. They soon quieted under the glaring stares of the adults in the room.

Jessica smiled and continued, "And now I'd like to turn it over to our principal, Mrs. Lunsford."

The students applauded politely on cue from Mr. Buchanan while Jessica took the empty seat next to an obviously dumbfounded Maddy.

Mrs. Lunsford smiled, "It is my pleasure to introduce our student representatives for this year's writer's conference. Before I do so, however, I would like to thank the PTA for so generously agreeing to provide scholarships to cover all expenses for both representatives. We are indeed fortunate here at Chase Middle to have the support of a strong Parent Teacher Association. The students were selected based on grades, state writing test scores, and recommendations from at least two language arts teachers. Our students will be joining representatives from all area middle schools in Orlando for this regional event. It is quite an honor to be chosen and this was not an easy decision to make. First, I will introduce our alternate, who will attend in the event that one of our students is unable to go. This year's alternate is none other than our news anchor, Jessica Townsend. Jessica, will you step forward?"

Jessica rose and strode confidently toward Mrs. Lunsford, shook her hand and said "thank you" as she accepted a certificate. She smiled for the camera and returned to her seat.

Maddy admired Jessica's poise and felt her heart pounding in her chest. She was in a state of wild confusion wondering how Mr. Daniels could make such a huge mistake. Should she say something or just go along? She knew she wouldn't say anything, at least not until later and especially not in front of cameras. She watched Michael go up for his award. She saw his mother beaming in the back of the class. And then she heard Mrs. Lunsford say,

"Now this last presentation will come as something of a surprise to the student since she is not aware of her parent's decision, but with their permission we decided to surprise her; Madison Schmidt, would you please step forward?"

Maddy rose, walked to Mrs. Lunsford, nervously shook her hand, accepted a certificate, and returned to her seat to the sound of the applause of her classmates. As the applause died down Jessica stood to do her wrap-up. Maddy didn't hear it; something in the back of her mind was clouding her thinking.

By the time the video crew had packed up and the seats were returned to their usual positions most of the class period was spent. Michael's mother and the principal left and Mr. Daniels decided against trying to present any material in the time remaining. Michael and Maddy sat together still trying to take it all in. Michael was sure the whole thing had been master-minded by his mother.

"You know it was okay in elementary school when she was always there because lots of other moms were around, too, but it's really getting old. Is she going to be lurking in the halls at my high school too? And why does everything have to be a big production? What does this stupid certificate say anyway? Congratulations on being chosen for something you're going to do in November? Last year they just read the names out during the morning announcements," he ended with a sigh.

Maddy wasn't sure what to say, she could tell he was upset. She looked at her certificate for the first time: "In recognition of superior achievement in writing skills."

"I guess they just wanted to have a visible symbol for the camera," she offered.

"Maybe next year they'll name it! Some lucky student will win the coveted *Golden Pen Prize,* or, *The Feather Quill Award*; that would tickle my mother's fancy," he suggested bitterly.

Jessica joined them, "Wasn't that a hoot? And we even got to miss having an actual class. Congratulations! So Maddy, was it really a surprise?"

"Yes, it was," she said simply, "in fact I want to ask Mr. Daniels a question now that things have calmed down."

Mr. Daniels smiled as she approached, "I've been waiting to hear from you; were you surprised?"

"Yes, I – I'm still not sure..." she couldn't find words.

"I left a message for your dad this morning during my planning period to tell him about the scholarship. He returned the call shortly after and we talked it over. He was very pleased, but still concerned about sending you so I told him that he or your mom could chaperone if they would feel more comfortable that way. After that he readily gave his permission."

"You t-told him he could be a chaperone? But, but I thought ..."

She wasn't sure but she thought Mr. Daniels looked slightly uncomfortable. "Well, it seems that I may have been mistaken about chaperones when I spoke to Mrs. Evans."

"So, one of my parents will be a chaperone?"

"I don't know; he's going to think about it and talk it over with your mom. I asked him to let me know by Friday if possible."

"Mr. Daniels, does Michael's mom know about the chaperone thing?"

"Well, uh, I thought I'd wait to hear from your parents before I mentioned anything. It really is better if students attend the conference without distractions, if possible."

Maddy smiled at him. She wouldn't say a word. She knew how to keep a secret.

Chapter 9

Scoop du jour

MADDY, MICHAEL AND Jessica sat together as usual for lunch. Jessica was excited enough for all of them. For her it was all a grand scoop; as the news anchor she had been the first student let in on the surprise. She simply loved the idea of being the first to know. She also loved the spotlight and as anchor she enjoyed breaking the news on camera. This was definitely a red-letter day for her; although it did not escape her notice that she, as the alternate, was far more excited than the chosen representatives.

"What is wrong with you two? I thought you'd be more excited," she said.

Michael was happy to hear that Maddy would be allowed to go, but he was still brooding about his mother. Sometimes he worried that she pulled strings to make things happen for him. Maybe he wouldn't have been selected without pressure from her in some way. He didn't think his writing was that good although he did receive high marks on the state exam.

As for Maddy, when she wasn't worrying that her dad would change his mind, she worried over the chaperone issue. If one of her parents did decide to chaperone then Michael's mother might insist on going as well which would ruin it for Michael. She couldn't imagine her father acting as a chaperone, he had never volunteered for anything at school before. Her mother was a more likely candidate, but would the scholarship cover her expenses too? She was sure Mr. Daniels hadn't thought about that.

"Hello, anybody home?" It was Jessica. "What is up with you guys today?"

Michael spoke first, he was candid as usual. "Well, I didn't see Maddy's or your parents there, but my dear ole mom seemed to be in the know."

"She's the President of the PTA and they are paying for the trip. Makes sense to me," said Jessica. Then, seeing the look on Michael's face, added, "I think your mom means well, Michael. Have you tried to talk to her about how you feel? Maybe you could point out you don't see many other parents at the school or something."

"I've tried, but it just seems to make her more determined. She thinks parents should be more involved at school; she complains that after elementary school most parents become less and less involved. She wonders what's wrong with everyone else."

"But have you tried to tell her how you feel about it?" Jessica was nothing if not direct.

"Not really," admitted Michael.

"How's that working for you?"

"What are you? A junior psychologist?"

Jessica ignored Michaels' remark and turned her attention to Maddy. "I didn't even know you'd been selected. Why keep good news a secret?"

"Let it go, Jess," said Michael.

"No, it's okay, Michael. Because I'm still not sure my dad won't change his mind and not let me go. Of course, that should make you happy as the alternate."

"Me? Oh, I don't want to go; it sounds like a lot of work! Crap! You mean I might have to actually go to this thing?"

For the first time since he had seen his mother, Michael smiled a genuine smile.

Chapter 10

Highs and lows

MADDY WAS SURPRISED by her parents' new found enthusiasm for her achievement.

Dinner that evening was a festive occasion with her father explaining that Mr. Daniels' call had been fielded by his supervisor at the department store where he worked selling electronics. His supervisor was not only impressed by his daughter's achievement, but his own daughter had participated in the Young Writer's Conference two years earlier so he knew a lot about it and said it was a "wonderful opportunity that only a *fool* would turn down". When he heard that Maddy had earned a "scholarship" that would pay expenses he was even more impressed. Maddy's father was glowing with pride after a day filled with receiving congratulations as the news about his daughter had spread through the store.

"So, I guess I was a bit hasty. I called your teacher back and when he offered to allow one of us to chaperone, I realized how badly he must want you to go," he concluded.

"We're very proud of you, dear," added her mother.

"Dad, about the chaperone thing; Mr. Daniels needs to know by Friday if one of you will want to chaperone," she decided she might as well find out right away.

"Well, I can't, of course, since I have to work and your mother has Cassie to take care of. What do you think, hon?"

"I really don't think they would want a five-year-old along," she offered.

Cassie had looked up at the mention of her name.

Maddy decided to take a chance. "Mr. Daniels has mentioned a few times that the conference officials prefer that the participants work with as few distractions as possible. I'm afraid they might think of Cassie as a distraction." *That was true enough.*

Since Cassie had no idea what a "distraction" might be she took no offense and although she was now paying more attention to the conversation she did not interrupt.

"No, I don't think we will be able to chaperone after all. I want you to be sensible while you're gone. Stay with the group and don't talk to anyone not associated with the conference," instructed her father.

"I won't," she assured him, "Did you know that everyone will have a piece included in a real magazine and we'll all get a copy? And the very best might get published in the local paper! It's going to be so cool! Thanks, Dad, for letting me go."

"Go? Where are you going?" asked Cassie.

"I'm going to go to a special meeting for writers, but it's not for a long time," answered Maddy.

"Oh. I can write my name," she offered.

"Yes, I know you can and you print very neatly, too."

Cassie beamed at the compliment.

———◦———

CASSIE WAS SLEEPING soundly, but Maddie was still awake thinking about the conference when she heard the door open quietly. She closed her eyes and pretended to be asleep while he came in and sat next to her on the bed. Soon she felt the familiar back rub under her pajama top.

"So I guess you're excited about the conference, huh?" he hissed.

"Huh, uh, yes," she tried to sound sleepy.

"Hey, I think you owe me a thank-you hug for letting you go on this writer's conference," he whispered. It was important to both of them to be quiet so Cassie would continue to sleep.

She complied. She knew this was his way of getting her to turn over. It was his usual routine. As she lay on her back he began stroking inside her thighs gently. When he removed her panties, she shifted her weight so he could pull them down. She knew it was too much to hope that he would go away now. She stared at the crack in the door, focused on the thin sliver of light from the hallway and dissolved until it would be safe to return.

Chapter 11

The Morning After

MADDY AWOKE WITH A tremendous headache. To allow for a few more minutes of quiet she decided to get herself ready for school before waking Cassie. At last she could wait no longer and gently woke her sister. She was grateful when Cassie woke easily and in her usual good humor. Cassie brushed her teeth while Maddy got out her clothes. She helped brush her hair, listening patiently to Cassie's chatter in spite of the pounding in her head.

They went to the kitchen where Maddy popped two slices of bread into the toaster. It was too early for her father to be up, but she knew her mother would sleep in this morning also. It was all part of the pattern. Cassie did not seem to notice. She ate her toast and drank her milk while Maddy made bologna sandwiches for their lunches.

"Come on, Cassie, I'll walk you to school," she said when it was time to go.

"I don't want to walk," pouted Cassie.

"You'll have to this morning," returned Maddy wearily.

"Why can't Mommy drive me?" she whined.

"Do you see Mommy anywhere?" Maddy snapped and then recovered, "It's just a couple of blocks and only big girls get to walk without their mommies."

"I want to go to school with Mommy," said Cassie unhappily. Maddy smiled and thought of Michael who would gladly argue the point.

At school Maddy headed straight for Mr. Daniel's room. It occurred to her that this was beginning to become a routine. She hurried hoping she would not see Michael, or especially his mother, until after she had told Mr. Daniels that her parents did not want to chaperone.

Mr. Daniels was grading papers at his desk. He smiled and waved her in. She waited for him to finish writing a comment on a paper next to a grade of B+. Then he looked up and she knew she had his full attention.

"Good morning, Maddy," he said cheerfully.

"Good morning. I just wanted to let you know that my parents have decided not to chaperone after all," she said smiling.

Mr. Daniels looked relieved. "That's good news. I'm not sure what I would have done if they had said yes."

Maddy was not sure what that meant exactly but decided not to ask. She knew Mr. Daniels had fibbed to either Mrs. Evans or her dad, but she couldn't decide which one and had no desire to pursue the topic. She held on to her firm belief that Mr. Daniels was a good teacher and a good person and she imagined that whatever he did, it was always in an effort to help his students. Still, the idea of him deliberately lying to a parent was slightly unsettling.

"So, are you beginning to get excited about the conference, now?" he asked.

"Yes," she smiled.

"Glad to hear it, see you fourth period," he said and she left at the sound of the first bell.

Maddy had Physical Science first period, her least favorite subject. Today's class had been mercifully easy on her headache as they streamed a video presentation on Newton's laws of motion. She closed her eyes and listened but did not watch the animated sequences demonstrating soccer balls in motion and soccer balls being acted on by someone's foot. She heard her classmates chuckle at the comments of the soccer ball in question, who apparently had a face and could talk. All in all, it was better than listening to Mr. Ernst teach. Accustomed to the pain of frequent headaches, she could usually work in spite of them. Still, it was good to see the room set up for a video.

The morning show was aired during the last twelve minutes of 1st period. Since she was featured, she roused herself enough to watch. It was embarrassing to see herself collect her certificate. There was Jessica poised at the microphone, speaking clearly and looking directly into the camera without even consulting her notes. There she was striding confidently to meet Mrs. Lunsford. And there was Michael mugging for the camera and winking to his friends as he collected his certificate. Maddy wondered at his ability to play his part even when she knew he was steaming about his mother. And there she was skulking over, head down, looking at her shoes and mumbling something unintelligible. She could feel her face turning red as she watched herself, but luckily no one else seemed to care. Many of the students were not even watching the program. She couldn't blame them: she was usually reading a book herself. Her teacher, Mr. Ernst, was watching today's show however and he brightened at the mention of one of his own. When the show was over he approached her, "Way to go Maddy!" he said with a smile, "It's always good to see the quiet, hard-working ones get their due."

Fourth period arrived and Maddy's headache showed no sign of letting up. Mr. Daniels gave the class an easy warm up exercise involving anagrams. He asked them to write their name at the top of a sheet of paper and see how many words they could find using the letters of their name. Maddy wrote Maddy Schmidt at the top of the page instead of her full given name. With her headache, Sarah Madison Schmidt was just too much to deal with. When time was called to end the exercise all she had on her paper were the words "my dad" under her first name. Mr. Daniels did not collect the exercise, he simply walked the room to see what his students had come up with. At Maddy's desk he stopped.

"Coming up dry?" he asked.

Maddy shrugged, "I guess so."

"Well, "Schmidt" is a bit heavy on the consonants," he admitted with a smile and went on to the next desk.

Maddy stared at the paper in front of her. When Mr. Daniels asked the students to take out their literature text book she ripped the offensive sheet of paper from her note book and wadded it up angrily.

Chapter 12

Plan of Attack

MICHAEL WAS STEWING. He was sitting in his room on his bed with his books piled beside him. He had a very spacious desk that he refused to use for homework mostly because it bugged his mom. His work space was equipped with computer and scanner. The walls were decorated with various video game posters and a string of Yankee pennants each commemorating a league or World Series championship. His video game corner was his favorite place in the room. The corner hutch was organized with rows of neatly arranged video games separated by game system. He was the proud owner of three gaming systems, all neatly hooked up to the 40-inch LED TV that sat in the center of the hutch. Also part of the set up was an old leather recliner, which when partly reclined put him at perfect eye level with the TV screen. It was his pride and joy.

Michael was not enjoying the finer features of his room, however; he had been trying to come up with a way to approach his mother about her frequent appearances at school. He didn't want to hurt her feelings; he knew she meant well. Still, he had taken Jessica's comments to heart and decided that the problem just wouldn't go away because he wanted it to. He was going to have to confront her. This would not be easy. His mother had an uncanny ability to miss the point entirely. If, for instance, he told her that he was being teased as a "momma's boy", she would want to know who was doing the teasing and head straight down to school to see what could be done about it. He wouldn't use this angle anyway because it wasn't really true; he was only very mildly teased and he handled those situations easily with his good nature and sense of humor. It was tempting to try it though, since it would be easier to complain about the imaginary bullies at school than speak directly with the cause of his consternation.

Several weeks had passed since his initial resolve and still he had taken no action. He had not progressed much further than the early planning for his offensive. He kept imagining his mother crushed from his remarks, bewildered by his inability to understand that she was working in his best interests. He flinched at the idea of causing her unhappiness and began to make excuses to himself for his inaction. *Today is not a good day; she's all stressed out about the budget meeting for her women's club. I don't want to upset her before she meets with the decorator to redo Dad's office.* Deciding to wait until after her birthday had bought him two guilt-free weeks.

Meanwhile, she had made no fewer than eleven unscheduled visits to the school in addition to her regular Wednesday morning volunteering in the school library. He had begun to keep track of dates and reasons for her visits as though building up a portfolio of evidence to use against her. He even considered enlisting his dad's help, but eventually abandoned the idea as even more hurtful than trying to confront her on his own. Although his parents usually got along just fine, this issue had come up between them in the past. He had overheard one particularly heated argument on the subject and had no wish to repeat the experience.

And so it was on this Thursday afternoon that he sat in his room trying to remember Jessica's original question. She had asked if he had ever tried to talk to her about it. No, it was: had he told her how it made him feel? Then he had teased her calling her a junior psychologist for her trouble. So now he considered the question: how did he feel about it? This was not as easy to determine as he thought it should be. He never thought about his feelings, he just felt them!

He opened the small blue notebook he had used to record his mother's visits.

———————⊙———————

SEPT. 26 RETURNED A book borrowed from the school library

Sept. 27 library visit to ask about the book fair, you just saw her yesterday, Ma!

Sept. 29 spoke to Mr. C about math grade- don't worry I'll pull it up to an A

Oct. 4 checked lunch card balance in the cafeteria - over **$30.00**

Oct. 7 asked guidance office for a list of electives for *next year*

Oct. 10 brought jacket – totally unnecessary!!

Oct. 13 asked principal about SAC recommendations??

Oct. 17 brought donuts to the teacher's break room

Oct. 20 discussed a dangerous situation with car pool lane to Officer Betts

Oct 24 brought my science paper- not finished yet! And not due until next week!!

Oct 28 asked Mr. D. if I need to do anything to prepare for the conference

———————⊙———————

NOW IT WAS A LITTLE easier to get in touch with his feelings. He shook his head as he went over the list. Most of the visits were unnecessary. For example, he could have returned the library book and checked on his lunch card balance himself. He did not need his jacket delivered as if he were in kindergarten and he was certainly capable of keeping track of when his assignments were due on his own. The conversations with Officer Betts, Mr. D. and Mrs. Lunsford could have been handled by phone. Probably the only welcome visit was the donut delivery.

So how did he feel? Annoyed. He continued to examine his feelings amused by an image of Jessica sporting a mustache and shiny bald head. "Anything else?" asked "Dr." Jessie. No, 'annoyed' just about said it all. "Why are you annoyed?" pressed Dr. Jessie. Hmmm, he looked again at his list, turned the page, and began to make more notes:

———◉———

SEPT. 26 EITHER YOU didn't trust me to return it for you, or you just wanted to be at school

Sept. 27 Since you just saw her, this was just an excuse to come on campus again.

Sept. 29 Would it kill you if I got, God forbid, a B in math?

Oct. 4 Didn't trust me to know when I might need more lunch money

Oct. 7 Planning my life for next year already?

Oct. 10 I'm old enough to know when I need my jacket.

Oct. 13 Committee stuff???

Oct. 17 Donuts – ok teachers like donuts

Oct. 20 Car pool lane - whatever

Oct. 24 Again, I know when my stuff is due without my mommy!

Oct. 28 Please try not to turn the fun stuff into work.

———————⊙———————

OKAY, THE PICTURE IS coming in more clearly now. I am upset because you are not letting me take care of business on my own. Don't you have any confidence in me? So, I feel angry and upset and I even know why I'm feeling this way. How can I find a way to talk to her about it?

Finally he decided he had spent enough time with his feelings and decided to leave his problem unsolved for the present. He tossed the notebook onto his bed and headed downstairs to the kitchen for a snack and checked the time to consider his TV viewing options. He wasn't sure but he thought Dr. Phil reruns might be on.

Chapter 13

Read it and Weep

AFTER A FEW MINUTES watching Dr. Phil, Michael switched the channel. Cartoons were much more to his liking than watching families argue over finances. After allowing himself a nice, long delicious cartoon break he decided to resume work on his science paper for a while.

Michael returned to his room to find his mother seated on the edge of his bed thoughtfully paging through his little blue notebook.

"Mom?"

"Yes?" she looked up at Michael as though seeing him in a new light.

"What are you doing?"

"Well, I came in to put away some laundry and decided to straighten up, when I noticed your little book. I thought it might be notes for your science project, but – uh – it isn't."

"Mom, I'm not doing a science project, just a paper."

"Oh."

"Did you read it?"

"Yes, I guess I did."

"All of it?"

"Just about."

Michael sighed. "I'm sorry, I never meant for you to see it. I was using it to try to find out why it bugs me to see you at school all the time – seems like almost every day."

"Have you been talking to your dad about this?"

"No," he answered quickly, "I've been trying to find a way to talk to *you*."

"Well, you found it."

"No, you did. You found it and you read it."

"I guess you're angry."

"No teenager wants to catch their mom going through their things. What about my privacy?" This last comment was a mere teenage formality, Michael was not overly concerned about his parents finding anything they shouldn't and privacy had never been a problem for him until this very moment.

"I am sorry about snooping, Michael. I hope you believe me when I say I've never done this before. I may follow you wherever you go, but I never snoop behind your back. This was an accident, but once I realized what it was I couldn't stop reading it. It was a real eye-opener."

"What do we do now?"

"Well, I guess we have to talk about it."

"Okay, hey Ma, is there any way you could cut down on the school visits?"

She smiled at his attempt to lighten the mood. "I'll try. I want to continue to volunteer on Wednesdays. It wouldn't be right to just quit without notice."

"Okay."

"I didn't realize how much I was babying you. I just want to be considered an active, involved parent."

"Well, you definitely have that reputation!"

"No, I'm afraid my reputation might be that of an overly involved nutcase with too much time on her hands."

"Well, that's a bit harsh."

"How long has this been bothering you, Michael?"

"I'm not sure, it was a gradual thing."

"Do the kids tease you about me?"

"No," he replied honestly, "they really don't."

"Have your teachers said anything about it?"

"No Mom; it's not about the other kids or the teachers – it's about *me* and how I feel about it."

"How do you feel?"

"You read the notebook."

"So you're content to just let the notebook cover the topic?"

"It shows how I feel."

"Yes, it shows me that you are angry. I can tell from the sarcasm in your remarks."

Michael sighed again; he was going to have to say it out straight. "Mom, I'm more frustrated than angry. It's like you don't think I can take care of the everyday business of being a middle school student on my own. It's not that hard, I can do it just like all the other kids do. Besides, kids forget their lunch money, have overdue library books and turn in assignments late all the time and they all manage to survive."

She nodded. "Okay. I'll work on this. I have just one more point to make before I leave the topic."

"What's that?"

"I hate it when you call me "Ma". Honestly, Michael, we're not hillbillies!"

They both smiled. Now, that didn't hurt – much.

Chapter 14

Jessie Speaks

"WELL, IT'S ONLY A FEW days until "Mike and Maddy's Big Adventure", said Jessica at lunch on Monday, "Are you getting excited?"

"I guess so," replied Maddy, "It hasn't really sunk in yet."

"Have you started packing?" asked Jessica.

"Packing? It's only pajamas, underwear, and a couple of tee shirts – how long can it take?" asked Michael.

"I'm sure your mother will take care of everything in your case," snipped Jessica.

"No, I beg to differ. Everything in my suitcase will be packed by yours truly!" returned Michael.

"Ooooh, do I sense a change in Mikie?" Jessica leaned forward eagerly.

"I did finally talk with my mom," answered Michael.

"Really! When?" asked Jessica and Maddy together.

"Yesterday, after school."

"So what happened?" asked Jessica, "Do you think she really heard you?"

"Yeah, I think I came through loud and clear," said Michael.

"How did she take it? I mean was she upset or anything?" asked Maddy.

"She took it pretty well, I think. I mean I thought she'd be crushed and hurt, but she didn't cry or yell or anything."

"Well, I guess it'll be easy enough to see if it worked; we'll just count the number of times we see her on campus this week," said Jessica.

"She said she won't quit Wednesdays at the library, but I think she'll try to cut down on other visits to school."

"I can't believe you actually did it, Michael," said Maddy impressed. "Was it hard?"

"Yes," said Michael simply. He wished he could talk to Maddy alone. He wasn't about to admit to Jessica how the conversation had really come about. He hadn't intended for his mother to read his notebook, but he wondered if he would have ever found a way to bring up the subject if she hadn't. It seemed too indirect and somehow cowardly to have accomplished his goal in this manner. Rather like a teenage girl deliberately leaving her diary out for her mother to read. Still, he was glad he could report to Jessica that he had done it, even though he preferred to skip over the details.

Of course Jessica needed all the gory details. "So tell me everything," she insisted.

"What's there to tell?" asked Michael, "I just asked her to cut down on school visits and she said she didn't realize they were bothering me."

"Well, if it was that easy, why didn't you do it a lot sooner?" asked Jessica.

"If I had known I would have," returned Michael dryly.

"I hope it works out. It might be harder for her to stop than she thinks. It's like breaking a bad habit – easier said than done," offered Maddy.

"Yeah, I know what you mean. At least she knows how I feel and she even apologized so I think she heard my side."

"That's so cool, imagine actually talking to a parent and being heard," said Maddy, "Will wonders never cease?"

"You ought to try it sometime yourself, Maddy," suggested Jessica.

"Why should I?" asked Maddy, surprised that the focus of the conversation was suddenly on her.

"Maybe you can get your dad to ease up on his stupid overnight rule. Since he let you do the conference, maybe he'll let you out for other things. I was thinking about having a get together over the Christmas break," invited Jessica.

"I'm not expecting miracles just because he's letting me go to one conference. In fact, I'm still worried he might change his mind," replied Maddy.

"Lord, I hope not," winced alternate Jessica.

"Me, too," agreed Maddy.

Jessica was still not ready to give up. "If talking it out worked for Michael it could work for you," she insisted.

Maddy did not like the direction this conversation was taking. She had hoped that she might distract Jessica with the threat of having to serve as alternate. She decided to try to refocus the topic back to Michael and his mom. "I don't think so. You just can't compare Michael's mother and my father -—it's like apples and oranges."

"More like bananas and melons, or, steak and spam," offered Michael.

"Who's the steak and who's the spam?" asked Maddy smiling.

"I'll never tell," replied Michael with a wink.

Jessica sighed and shook her head. They were not taking her suggestion seriously and she knew it.

"Well, I guess if it doesn't bother you to live under a dictatorship, okay," she said, obviously miffed.

"It's not a dictatorship," said Maddy equally disgruntled.

"What would you call it? You have zero freedom. You can't go to sleepovers or slumber parties. You weren't allowed to join Girl Scouts when a bunch of us did because we go on overnight camp outs and you couldn't join the soccer team even when the coach was practically begging you to try out. You really don't get out much, do you?" Jessica ended sarcastically.

Maddy sighed. Even though it was all true she was beginning to feel angry at Jessica for what seemed like an attack all of a sudden.

"It wasn't just the overnight stuff with scouts and soccer, Jessica. Uniforms and dues are expensive and since we only have one car I can't always be sure I'll have a ride when I need one. Besides I didn't really want to join the scouts anyway."

"Well, you definitely wanted to be on the soccer team. You play well and we could've really used you and you know the team would've made sure you had a ride. And there are only overnights if we make the finals, but of course, we didn't," finished Jessica bitterly. She had finally run out of steam.

"Well, I don't know what to tell you Jessica," returned Maddy, sadly.

Michael had listened with interest. He already knew how Jessie felt about the soccer team and how angry she was when Maddy didn't even try out. Jessie was competitive and hungry for a winning season. Their team was pretty good, but never quite seemed to make the playoffs. The addition of Maddy just might have made them good enough to make the finals this year. And

Jessie was right: Maddy wanted very much to play soccer with the team. What he had never actually realized was how restricted Maddy really seemed to be. It wasn't just sleepovers; when he thought about it he realized that aside from school Maddy didn't have any outside activities. No dance class, music lesson, sports team, clubs, or anything. She rarely attended parties even if they weren't sleepovers and she never invited anyone home with her. He wondered briefly how she filled the time during summer vacation. He also knew his role in this scenario. His two friends were upset and he was there to provide a light moment of humor to bring them all back together. Unfortunately, this time nothing humorous came to mind.

"Tell her you'll think it over," he suggested softly.

Chapter 15

Preparations

MADDY WAS CONSIDERING which sweater to pack. Although the weather in Orlando was seasonably pleasant, she was planning for the "indoor weather". Sometimes the air conditioning could be uncomfortably cold indoors in hotel meeting rooms. Jessica had warned her of this possibility and even loaned her a pretty light pink sweater decorated with delicate beads. The two of them had arrived at a sort of truce after their lunchtime disagreement. Maddy knew that the sweater was Jessica's way of making amends. She smiled as she decided to pack Jessie's sweater and keep her dark brown cardigan with her on the bus.

"What are you doing?" asked Cassie.

"Packing a bag for my trip," replied Maddy.

"When are you going?"

"Tomorrow morning and I'll be back on Saturday."

"Can I go?"

"No, sorry sweetie, I wish you could."

Their mother appeared in the doorway. "Do you have everything? I could throw in a load of wash if you want to take something that isn't clean."

"No, I think I've got it."

"I wish you had a robe to take."

"I won't need one."

"What time are you meeting the bus?"

"Seven-thirty at the Cookson Mall. Michael and his mom are picking me up at seven."

"You'll have get up even earlier than on a regular school day," observed her mother.

"Yeah, but I've never ridden on a charter bus before, so it'll be easy to get up."

"What's a charter bus?" asked Cassie.

"It's just a big bus, but Jessica says sometimes they have TVs with movies playing and there's even a bathroom right on the bus!" answered Maddy.

"Do you get to pick the movie?" asked Cassie.

"I don't know how it works, but I'll tell you when I get back."

"Remember to call us when you arrive," reminded her mother.

"I won't forget. Michael said I could use his phone to call."

"Good, now wash up. Dinner will be ready soon."

Maddy noticed that her mother seemed tense. She began to worry that her dad might withdraw his permission at the last minute. This thought had been flitting through her head for days, she would push it away each time, but sooner or later it would come sneaking back. It was the reason she had waited until the very last day to pack her bag. She decided not to bring up the trip that evening unless someone else did.

Dinner was spaghetti and meatballs, one of her dad's favorite meals. Her mother's effort to make the evening go smoothly was not lost on Maddy. Cassie amused everyone with her efforts to consume the long slippery strands of pasta. She refused offers to cut them into smaller pieces just as she refused all suggestions. She had seen her dad expertly spin the strands onto his fork and she worked and worked to master the technique without much success.

That didn't stop her from continuing to try and she had seemingly endless patience as she clumsily turned her fork. By the time vanilla ice cream was served for dessert her face was covered from cheek to cheek in orange pasta sauce.

Maddy volunteered to clean up Cassie after dinner. She thought she might spend the evening entertaining her with the hope that they might both avoid their father.

She spent almost an hour on her bath, scrubbing stubborn spaghetti sauce from her cheeks and spending a long time washing her hair. She even put conditioner on it as a special treat. Cassie didn't care much about soft, shiny hair but she delighted in the way it smelled of strawberries.

After her bath Maddy carefully and patiently combed out her hair and braided it into two long, thick braids. This was a treat for both of them since Maddy loved to play with her sister's hair and Cassie loved the attention. It would also save her mother from having to fuss with her hair in the morning. Their mother did not share Maddy's enthusiasm for hair styling and was much less careful about not pulling too much with the comb. This way, it would already be done and if Cassie kept the braids in until Friday morning, she could then unbraid them herself and they should comb out easily. As she worked she explained all this to Cassie who nodded solemnly and agreed to Maddy's plan.

"Mommy hurts my head sometimes," she asserted.

"She doesn't mean to," soothed Maddy.

"She gets mad at my hair," insisted Cassie.

"Your hair can be a lot of work and sometimes Mommy doesn't have time for it," explained Maddy.

"She wanted to get it cut short, but Daddy said no," revealed Cassie.

"She did?" asked Maddy, surprised.

"Yep, but Daddy said she better not because it's too pretty," said Cassie proudly.

"Oh, I see," said Maddy.

"He called me Lovely Long Locks," added Cassie smiling happily.

"Really?" asked Maddy.

"Yes. Maddy, what are locks?" wondered Cassie.

"Locks are hair, like Goldilocks. She has long, pretty golden hair," explained Maddy.

"Oh, I get it," said Cassie understanding, "maybe Daddy can call me Brownilocks!"

"Maybe," said Maddy impressed with Cassie's quick grasp of the new word.

After Cassie's bath they spent the evening in their room. Maddy worked on a few assignments for classes she would miss over the next two days and double checked the contents of her overnight bag more than once. Cassie entertained herself with Barbie dolls pretending they were packing for an overnight trip. She had all their tiny clothes laid out on her bed and used one of her own tiny purses as their suitcase. She even had their tiny bottle of sun screen and little plastic camera ready to go. Maddy was impressed with her characteristic attention to detail.

At nine o'clock their parents came in to tell Cassie to get to bed which was Maddy's cue to take her shower for the evening. As she locked herself in the bathroom she breathed a sign of relief – only ten hours to go. Still, she wouldn't believe it until she was sitting on that bus as it rolled out of the parking lot.

Later as she lay in bed she waited, wondering. She slipped into her regular daydream, expecting the door to crack open silently at any moment. In her daydream she is sitting in her English class when the principal comes in and whispers something to Mr. Daniels. She imagines Mr. Daniels' eyes filled with concern as he rises to approach her. She imagines Jessica wide-eyed with the anticipation of breaking news. She sees Michael sit up as Mr. Daniels touches her shoulder protectively and asks her to come with him into the hall with the principal. They gently tell her that there has been an accident. Usually, she just kills off her dad, but sometimes both parents die in a tragic car accident. Tonight she decides that only her dad needs to die.

She accepts condolences from friends, attends the funeral, consoles Cassie, and vows to help her mother with the housework since she will need to find a job. She imagines all this in great detail all the time wondering vaguely why the door doesn't open. Her happy daydream continues until true dreams come.

Chapter 16

Free at last

MICHAEL, TRUE TO HIS word, had packed his own bag much to his mother's dismay. Knowing she would need more time to adjust to his declaration of semi-independence, he gave in on the issue of socks and underwear – packing an extra pair of each just in case, but steadfastly refused to include an entire back up outfit slightly more formal than the khaki slacks and polo shirt he had in mind. He knew she was imagining him collecting some kind of special award at the end of the conference and wanted him to dress the part. He smiled to himself as he imagined her secreting one of those tweed jackets with the patches on the elbows into a hidden compartment in his suitcase.

"Did you remember your toothbrush and toothpaste?" she asked.

"Yes, I did, Mother," replied Michael with just a touch of annoyance.

"Fine, just don't forget your ticket for the bus and your cell phone, *with charger*," she added in spite of his tone.

"I have them," he answered and then quickly stuffed his charger in an outer pocket of his bag.

"Okay, we're ready then. Do you know how to find Maddy's house?" she asked.

"I have her address, she's on Jefferson Avenue near the school; we should be able to find it easily enough."

"Oh, dear, you haven't been there before?"

"Well, no, do you remember ever taking me there?" *What a silly question, Mother, it's not as if I drive a car.* "She walks to school, it can't be that hard to find and we know where Jefferson is."

"I just don't want to be late and miss the bus; I hope she's ready when we get there," she worried.

"She will be," assured Michael. If there was one thing he was certain about it was that Maddy would be ready to go and watching for their arrival. And so she was; she even had her bag sitting on the front steps. Maddy herself appeared beside it a moment later as his mother pulled into the driveway.

Michael hopped out to help her with her bag and then joined her in the back seat. They buckled up, all settled to go and... nothing.

"Mom?"

"Yes, dear?" His mother stared expectantly at the empty front porch.

"Uh, we're ready to go now."

"Maddy, aren't your folks coming out to say goodbye?" asked Mrs. Evans.

"No, ma'am, they're still sleeping." Maddy prayed for Mrs. Evans to back out of the driveway. She still half expected her father to appear on the porch and call her back inside having changed his mind.

"I see," said Mrs. Evans, although it was clear she did not see at all. Her lips were flattened into a thin straight line as she backed out slowly still watching the front door of the house as if willing it to open and spit out a caring and concerned parent.

Maddy considered trying to explain, but in the end decided that it would be best to say nothing, especially in light of the fact that she would find it almost impossible to explain the behavior of parents she didn't really understand herself.

Michael tried to help by choosing this moment to annoy his mother.

"See, Mom, Maddy's folks don't hover over her every move. I bet she even packed her bag all by herself without any input."

"Oh no, my mom offered to wash anything I might want to take that wasn't clean and she worried that I might forget something," said Maddy relieved to be able to truthfully demonstrate her mother's concern over her preparations.

"See, Michael, her mom was interested in helping her pack, too," interjected Michael's mom with a triumphant smile.

"Score a point for moms everywhere," returned Michael with mock annoyance.

Michael's mother, satisfied at last, slowly backed out of the driveway.

———◉———

THEY WERE EARLY AS Michael knew they would be. There were a handful of other parents and middle schoolers milling around the mostly empty parking lot of the shopping center. This was an unusual field trip for all the students since few of them knew one another unlike most class outings. Two students from each of the sixteen area middle schools made 32 students in all plus nine chaperones.

The parents were getting along famously, chatting easily among themselves. Some talked quietly sipping on drive-thru coffee while others conversed more distractedly frequently checking their watches and worrying about being late to work. All of them seemed genuinely happy about the adventure about to unfold for their talented offspring. Michael's mother joined the group of adults, while Michael and Maddy paced a short distance away.

The students were less eager to mingle. They sat quietly on the curb or hovered near their parents while still trying to appear independent of them. A few pulled out paperbacks and read. Maddy was glad she had Michael to talk to.

"Well, here we are twenty minutes early and no bus in sight," said Michael, "and my mom was absolutely certain we would be late."

"We would have been if she had waited for my parents to come out and say goodbye," muttered Maddy quietly.

"You should have seen her panicking about getting lost trying to find your house."

"She did? But I'm only two blocks from Chase; I walk to school."

"I know, but she always does that when she driving somewhere she hasn't been before. And she can't stand the idea of being late so, of course, we're unbelievably early. I would have killed for twenty more minutes of sleep."

"I was surprised I could sleep at all last night."

"Why?"

"I guess I'm still waiting for my dad to call the whole thing off. I was happy when they didn't get up to see me off. And it wasn't easy to get ready without waking my sister."

"It's funny, they were so strict about letting you go, but then they don't even want to say goodbye," observed Michael, "I can't decide if they are overprotective or what." In truth Michael had recently come to decide that the best adjective to describe Maddy's father was controlling, but refrained from saying so remembering how hurt Maddy had been when Jessie had used the word dictatorship to describe her family.

"Don't ask me to explain it, I don't understand it either."

"Here's the bus," observed Michael.

"It's early."

"That's good because it will take a while to get everyone boarded and organized," said Michael.

"I guess so, I wonder where the chaperones are," said Maddy.

"Don't know, Mr. Daniels told my mom that all the chaperones are teachers," offered Michael.

Maddy nodded. She had no intention of telling Michael that her parents were invited to be chaperones. She still couldn't decide if Mr. Daniels was bluffing when he offered or fibbing to Mrs. Evans when he told her she couldn't. She was waiting to see if all the adults really were teachers. She also didn't want to open the topic while Michaels's mother was within hearing.

The first chaperone to appear was a Miss Barber. She was a tiny woman with an important air about her. She wore a navy-blue business suit, dragged a suitcase with wheels and carried an accordion folder and clipboard with lists.

"Good morning!" she called smiling. "We have a lot to sort out so please listen carefully. Parents, the bus should be back in this parking lot between 11:30 am and noon on Saturday. Does everyone have the phone chain list? I have extra copies if you need one. The phone chain will only be used in case of emergency, or to notify you if the bus will be later than expected. Students, when I call your name please come forward with your school ID ready."

This last statement caused a mild stir as students began to dig for their IDs. One or two began to fret when they could not find it right away. Michael's mother was the first to step among the students to give him a quick farewell hug. Other parents followed her lead. Eventually everyone resettled to listen for their names. Boarding was done alphabetically so Michael was among the first to be called. Miss Barber searched for his permission slip in the accordion folder, checked his ID and handed his overnight bag to the driver to be loaded in the storage area under the bus. More chaperones showed up to assist with the process.

Finally, Maddy heard her name called, "Schmidt, Sarah Madison." She wound her way to the head of the line and gave her ID to the teacher who located her permission slip, took her suitcase, and smiled as he returned her ID card. It was Mr. Daniels.

Chapter 17

A New Secret

MICHAEL HAD SAVED HER a seat about one third of the way down the aisle. Maddy plopped her bookbag into her seat and shrugged out of her sweater. "Did you see who checked my ID?" she asked.

"Nope."

"It was Mr. Daniels."

"Really? Cool!"

"Yeah, that should make things interesting."

Maddy began to look around the bus. There were more than enough seats for everyone. The seats across the aisle were empty. She saw the flat screen hanging above the seat a few rows up. There were several of them spaced throughout the bus, just as Jessica had described. As she settled into her seat Miss Barber called for everyone's attention once again.

"We should arrive at our hotel at around 11:00 am. We'll check in and hand out room assignments at that time. After we check into our rooms we will meet in the courtyard of the hotel for a box lunch. Our first session will begin at 1:00. A few minutes after we are underway we'll pass out a snack. Any questions?"

"What about a movie?" shouted a voice from the back.

"Ah, a true scholar," commented Miss Barber. "The movie will begin shortly after we depart. I have no idea what it is so don't ask."

In the end almost no one watched the movie. Small conversations began as the students started to get acquainted. A couple of kids fell asleep. Every so often an adult would walk the aisle making sure all was well.

Maddy and Michael ate their snack: apple juice and shortbread cookies. "What are we in kindergarten?" remarked Michael. He searched his book bag until he found two small brown bags. He gave one to Maddy, who accepted looking surprised.

"They're from my mom, and she made one up for you, too. It has a granola bar, apple, small bag of chips and my personal favorite, a candy bar," he said with a wink.

"Wow, that was really nice of her," said Maddy thinking of Mrs. Evans in a new light.

"Yeah, she's not all bad," agreed Michael.

It was Mr. Daniels turn to walk the aisle. Hey, Mr. D.!" called Michael as he passed.

"Hello, Michael, Maddy," returned Mr. Daniels nodding to each of them in turn.

"Why didn't you tell us you were coming?" asked Michael.

"I didn't know myself until the last minute. One of the chaperones had to cancel and since I'm on the committee I got the call and here I am."

"So the kids at school are getting a sub," observed Michael, "glad I'm not there."

Mr. Daniels smiled and shook his head as he continued down the aisle.

"How do you do that?" asked Maddy.

"Do what?"

"Talk to teachers like that. You say stuff I'd never say."

"Like what?"

"Like, 'glad I'm not there.'"

"Oh. Was that bad?"

"Not really bad, I'd just never say that to a teacher," Maddy chuckled. She wished she could be so comfortable with the adults in her life.

"They're just people, they have a sense of humor, well, most of them do."

"I guess. How are things with your mother? I only saw her once this week and that was yesterday in the library for her weekly volunteering. That's pretty good."

"Yeah, she is trying."

"How did you do it; how do you start a conversation like that?"

"By accident," revealed Michael.

"Accident?" asked Maddy.

Michael then told her the whole story beginning with his notebook and ending with his mother's apology. Maddy was quiet, allowing him to tell the story in his own way without interruptions. She was mildly surprised that he didn't add his characteristically humorous details. She had a sense that he truly regretted the way their conversation had come about. When he was finished, she was thoughtful.

"Your mom is really something, Michael," she said finally, "she didn't yell or cry or even seem mad."

"No, but she did go kinda quiet which made me feel terrible."

"She apologized to you; it's even hard for me to imagine."

Michael was thoughtful for a moment. He had decided that he would like to try to explain his mother to Maddy. He wanted someone to know that she wasn't just some crazy over the top mother who hovered over his every move. He couldn't tell the guys at school and he wouldn't tell Jessie. It would be cruel to tell her and then ask her not to spread it around. He had a sense that Maddy could hear what he had to say without feeling the need to talk about it with anyone else.

"Maddy, can I tell you something personal?" he asked.

"I guess so," returned Maddy, interested.

"It's the sort of thing I wouldn't want everyone at school to know."

"Okay."

"I had a younger brother once, but only for a couple of days, I don't even remember him," said Michael.

Maddy was surprised by this revelation. She and Michael had been friends for four years and she always thought of him as an only child. She looked at Michael thoughtfully and asked, "What happened to him?"

"He died a few days after he was born. My dad told me he was born too soon and just wasn't strong enough..." he trailed off. "Anyway," he continued after a moment, "I don't even remember him; I was only two when he was born. My dad said my mom was heartbroken. I sometimes wonder if that's why she hovers so much."

"Think she's trying to mother you enough for two?"

"Maybe, I never thought of it that way," smiled Michael, "I just thought she was afraid she might lose me, too."

"That's sad," said Maddy, "but it explains a lot."

"Maddy," said Michael quietly, "I really hope you won't tell anyone else, not even Jessie."

"My lips are sealed." Now Maddy had another secret to keep.

Chapter 18

Alex

MADDY WAS ASSIGNED a room on the 8th floor overlooking the pool. Their room chaperone was a Miss DePaula, a Language Arts teacher from another middle school. She would sleep on a rollaway bed while the four girls shared the two queen sized beds. Her three roommates seemed nice enough. Maddy was to share a queen-sized bed with a girl named Alex. Her given name was Alexandra which she attributed to her parents' delusions of grandeur, but she said she preferred to be called Alex.

Maddy had never been in such a nice hotel. Her family vacations were always long car trips to stay with aunts and uncles. Motels were just places to pull off and sleep for a few hours before getting back on the road. She was surprised when Alex said she had stayed in a nearby hotel for a whole week once while her family visited the area theme parks. She had never imagined spending a whole week in a hotel!

After a few moments exploring the room, she and Alex went down to the courtyard for lunch. Maddy spotted Michael immediately and introduced him to Alex.

"Isn't this place fantastic?" asked Maddy.

"It's nice, I like the Hilton better, though. It has a great pool," said Michael.

"The best pool is at the Hyatt," enthused Alex, "it's like a lagoon with fake rocks and waterfalls."

"I've been there!" said Michael, "they have a rope bridge and two slides. But my favorite thing is the glass elevator."

"Is it pretty?" asked Maddy.

"Yeah, I guess, but the best thing is the drop, especially from the top. It's like a mini thrill ride. My mom hates it."

"It's not that good," objected Alex.

"Oh, I know, it's really nothing, but my mom thinks it is!" Michael laughed. Alex and Michael spent a few minutes debating the finer points of their favorite area hotels. Maddy quickly realized that the hotel they were in fell far below their usual standard of travel.

Maddy asked Michael to borrow his cell phone to let her parents know she had arrived safely. There was no answer so she left a message and gave them Michael's number in case they needed to call her.

Box lunches were handed out. Michael selected roast beef with a bag of corn chips and an apple. He compared it favorably to the below par snack handed out on the bus.

"This is more like it," he said chomping down on the crusty bread. Small flakes of crust rained down on his shirt. He brushed them away and continued eating with gusto. Maddy noted that Alex looked slightly embarrassed by his enthusiasm for the sandwich. She wondered if Alex might have expected more refined table manners from someone who held forth so competently during the great hotel amenities debate.

"May I have everyone's attention, please," announced Miss Barber. "In ten minutes we will meet in conference room C on the second floor. Food is not permitted in the conference rooms, so please finish your meals quickly. You don't need to bring anything with you, everything is provided, but please be on time.

The conference room was set up with all chairs facing forward. Maddy's first impression was a slight let down. Evidently "everything provided" meant chairs. She, Alex, and Michael took seats about three rows back and in the center of the row.

As soon as everyone had filed in and found seats the always prepared Mrs. Barber appeared again and began to hand out sheets of paper. It was an agenda of the conference. Maddy scanned it with interest.

———◉———

Workshop Schedule

DAY 1

   11:00 am Buses arrive Orlando

   11:30 am Check-in and box lunch

   1:00 pm Presentation - Mr. Paul Knowles

   1:30 pm Break into brain-storming groups

   2:30 pm Meet writing coach to develop topic

   3:00 pm Break

   3:30 pm Writing session

   5:30 pm Meet with writing coach for feedback

   6:00 pm Dinner (Ballroom C)

   7:00 pm Leisure activity

   9:00 pm Return to assigned room

   10:00 pm Lights out

———◉———

DAY 2

   8:00 am Breakfast in hotel restaurant

9:00 am Presentation - Mrs. Cynthia Patterson
9:30 am Writing session
11:30 am Meet writing coach for feedback
12:00 noon Lunch (Courtyard)
1:00 pm Complete final draft (**due by 5 pm**)
5:00 pm Leisure activity
7:30 pm Banquet and Special Presentations
9:30 pm Return to room
10:00 pm Lights out

DAY 3

8:00 am Breakfast in hotel restaurant
9:30 am Meet in lobby with luggage
10:00 am Buses depart
Do not be late for boarding!!!

SHE WISHED SHE HAD brought a pen at least, since so far, one had not been "provided". Alex and Michael appeared not to mind. Michael checked his agenda to find out when the next break would be and wondered aloud if a snack might be offered. Alex had scanned to the bottom of the page and worried if the outfit she had brought would be nice enough for the banquet. Maddy had not considered that a banquet would be part of the proceedings. She did not remember reading about it in her information packet.

"Did you know about a banquet?" she asked her companions.

"No," said Alex slightly dismayed.

"Nope," said Michael, "and I'm sure it wasn't in the information we got because if it was my mom would have insisted I pack a suit. Guess I dodged a bullet!"

"I didn't pack anything nice enough for a banquet," worried Maddy.

"We'll figure it out," Alex assured her.

Chapter 19

Brainstorming

MR. KNOWLES' LECTURE was only thirty minutes on the schedule, but somehow he managed to make it seem much longer. He had emphasized several key points: write about what you know; plan your writing; the importance of the introductory paragraph; how to add interesting details; and proofreading. Maddy was surprised to see that he had ended on time. Although she had listened and taken in the key points she had been distracted and spent much of the time going over everything she had packed trying to rearrange them into an outfit suitable for the banquet.

"He needs to take some of his own advice about adding interesting details; only the freezing temperature in the room kept me awake," grumbled Michael as they made their way to their assigned meeting room for the brainstorming session.

"How is it possible to make a lecture about making your writing a pleasure to read so boring?!" muttered Alex.

"Even Maddy wasn't paying attention," observed Michael, "which is almost unheard of!"

Maddy was surprised by this comment. She had not realized that Michael might have noticed how distracted she was. She felt herself redden and smiled self-consciously.

She started to object. "I was listening," she began, but then thought better of it and added, "well, a little."

"Exactly!" laughed Michael, "even you couldn't resist the urge to drift away under the sound of Knowles' mind-numbing narration!"

"Why, that's almost alliterative," smiled Maddy.

"What is?"

"Your 'numbing narration' description of Mr. Knowles' talk," answered Maddy.

"I still don't know what alliterative means," said Michael confused.

"Alliterative," explained Alex, "is where the beginning sounds of words repeat. Like Peter Piper picked a peck of pickled peppers."

"Never heard of it," said Michael.

"And yet, you make nice use of it intuitively," offered Maddy.

Alex rolled her eyes.

The brain-storming session was much more interesting. The students were divided into four groups of eight according to the way they had been seated in the lecture room. This allowed the threesome to remain together. This room was much smaller than the first and the chairs were arranged in a circle. Maddy was pleased to see Mr. Daniels come in. She was wondering if he would lead the brain-storming session, but he remained in the back of the room and sat on a bench outside the circle. After a few minutes another man entered the room. The students stirred with interest at his arrival. The first thing Maddy noticed was his height, he was not very tall, but had an athletic build. He had a dark complexion and thick black, wavy hair. Maddy thought he had a friendly way about him as she watched him introduce himself to Mr. Daniels. After a few minutes mingling with arriving students, he took the seat to her immediate right in the circle.

"Good afternoon, my name is Mr. Rodriguez, and I will facilitate this brain-storming session. Let's start with introductions. We'll go around the circle. Please give us your name, school, and one interesting fact about yourself that you would like to share with the group. I'll begin in order to give you all a chance to ignore me while you quickly think of what you plan to reveal to the group. Remember this is a brain storm; we'll think quickly, throw out ideas and see where they land. Button up your raincoats, I think I feel a change in the weather! As I said, my name is Mr. Rodriguez, I write feature articles for the Daytona Daily News and I do this as a volunteer at two conferences each year. I live near the beach in Daytona and love to surf whenever I can." He paused briefly before turning with a smile to the student seated on his right, and added "Let's begin with you."

Maddy's heart was pounding. She always became very nervous before speaking in a group, even a small group. What could she say about herself? She glanced at Michael who looked relaxed and truly interested for the first time that morning. She checked on Alex who seemed unconcerned as she calmly waited her turn. Maybe if she listened to the others she might come up with something. Surfing? That wasn't much help; neither were baseball, ballet, horseback riding, swimming, or poodles. It was Alex's turn.

"My name is Alexandra Feldman. I like to be called Alex. I am a student at Marston Middle School and I hope to be a neurosurgeon one day."

"Interesting," interjected Mr. Rodriguez.

"Hi, I'm Michael Evans, I go to Chase Middle School and I hate orthodontists, piano lessons and overzealous parental units."

"Very interesting," said Mr. Rodriguez. Mr. Daniels smiled and crossed his arms.

"My name is Sarah Madison Schmidt; my friends call me Maddy. I am a student at Chase Middle School and I actually enjoy my younger sister Cassie."

"Very good, all of you. A few of you, those who had a bit more time to plan, and I do hope to impress upon you the importance of planning, but as I was saying, a few of you broke the pattern that had begun with my mention of a hobby. Alex was the first to mention an aspiration rather than an experience or hobby. Michael turned the tables on us all by listing things he *doesn't* like. Maddy surprised us by revealing that she actually likes something we might expect her to dislike. Perhaps a few of you are now wishing you had thought to say something different or would like to repeat your original thought in a new way. Let's go around the circle again."

This time the group learned that the ballet student had performed in New York City, the poodle had won ribbons at several dog shows, and the baseball lover was an All-City All Star playing centerfield for his team. The swimmer changed his sound bite altogether to reveal that he hoped to design video games one day. The horseback rider revealed her ambition to become a pilot. Alex explained that her interest in the brain grew out of her experiences with her grandmother who suffers from both Parkinson's and Alzheimer's diseases. Michael offered that he'd like to have a go at stand-up comedy someday. Again, Maddy was somewhat distracted, although she was no longer worrying over an outfit for the banquet. She pushed down the negative thoughts that had arisen and forced herself to concentrate on the matter at hand. When her turn came she offered that she was an avid reader of fantasy and science fiction.

"Okay," said Mr. Rodriguez, "are any of you beginning to settle on a topic for your essay? One of the first rules of writing is to write about what you know. The piece you will write has only one requirement: it is to be a reflection of yourself. Who do we know better than ourselves and our own interests, desires, ambitions, and opinions? This time we will not go around the circle, instead I'll ask for volunteers who feel they might have decided on their topic. The group may then add their own suggestions. Once your topic is approved you may leave if you like, or stay to help others finalize their topics. Any volunteers?"

Alex's hand went up immediately. She wanted to examine how her relationship with her grandmother had changed as first Parkinson's and later Alzheimer's was stealing her away bit by bit. After some give and take with the group she decided not to focus as much on her ambition to become a doctor; her real message was to be the value of her relationship with a very special family member.

During the next call for volunteers three more hands went up. No one left early and everyone left excited about their topic. Michael and Maddy were the last to make their decisions. Michael finally decided to write about what he called his "wonderful wacky relationship" with his mother. Maddy knew that he would be able to make it both funny and touching. She also knew that his mother would love it even if some of the laughs were at her expense. She noticed how almost all the stories were becoming stories about people, not hobbies or accomplishments.

Maddy seriously considered writing her essay about how she almost didn't attend the conference. She shared with the group how she worried even to the last moments that her dad would change his mind. Michael was all for it. Mr. Rodriguez was cautiously optimistic. Mr. Daniel's head lifted with sudden interest. In the end, and after much deliberation and input from the group, she decided to stick with her first impulse to write about her relationship with her sister.

Chapter 20

Coach Rodriguez

WHEN THE BRAIN STORMING session ended the students were instructed to remain in the room. They waited while Mr. Rodriguez and Mr. Daniels pulled out the accordion folded walls on metal tracks and reconfigured the room into four much smaller ones. Meetings with writing coaches were to be one on one and were scheduled in fifteen-minute increments, so half the students would wait while the others were coached. Maddy, Alex, Michael and another student named John were then asked to wait in the hall while the first group met with their coaches. Soon three other adults joined Mr. Rodriguez. Mr. Daniels waited in the hall with the students.

"Mr. D., aren't you a coach?" Michael asked.

"No, I'm just a chaperone. I will get to help out when it comes time to proofread your essays, but for now I'm just observing," said Mr. Daniels.

"Not quite ready for prime time, eh?" said Michael.

"Michael!" Maddy was aghast.

"No, not quite," laughed Mr. Daniels, "the coaches have all had training to prepare them for the conference. Also, most of them are published writers. I guess I just don't quite qualify. So, are you happy with your topics?"

"I think I am," said Michael, "I mean I know I want to write about my mom, but I'm not sure exactly how to make it interesting."

"That's where the coaches will help you. Just remember, she's going to read it," pointed out Mr. Daniels.

"Don't worry, I'll definitely keep that in mind while I'm writing!" Michael assured him.

Maddy smiled thinking about how Michael's notebook fell into the wrong hands. She knew he wouldn't risk hurting his mother's feelings in writing a second time.

"So how about you, Maddy, how's your topic coming along?" asked Mr. Daniels.

"I don't know, yet," admitted Maddy.

"How old is your sister?" asked Mr. Daniels.

"Five," answered Maddy.

"That's, let's see, about eight years difference. Do you have other sisters or brothers?" asked Mr. Daniels.

"No, just Cassie and me," replied Maddy.

"So she's a lot younger than you; in five years when you're getting ready for college she'll be just ten," observed Mr. Daniels.

"Yeah, I guess so," said Maddy, "I hadn't really thought that far ahead."

"It'll be here before you know it. Of course by then, she probably won't need her big sister as much as she does now."

———— ◉ ————

IT WASN'T LONG BEFORE the first group of students filed out of the room exchanging ideas about their plans for their essays. When Maddy entered the room she saw Mr. Daniels conferring with Mr. Rodriguez. She hung back with the other students waiting for instructions about where to sit. Soon each student was approached by a coach and led to a table where paper and pens waited.

Maddy was assigned to Mr. Rodriguez which made her happy because she wouldn't have to meet someone totally new.

Mr. Rodriguez consulted his print out before addressing Maddy. "So, Sarah, uh, wait, you like to be called something else, right?"

"Yes," she smiled shyly and pointed to her name tag, "I like to be called Maddy."

"Okay, Maddy, remind me of your topic," said Mr. Rodriguez.

"I thought I might write about my sister, Cassie."

"Yes, I remember, you said, and I think this is a direct quote: "I actually enjoy my younger sister'. I remember because you made it memorable, even amusing. This is what we hope to continue with your essay."

Maddy felt encouraged by Mr. Rodriguez's comment. She had made it memorable! Even amusing! She wasn't amusing, Michael was amusing. But, Mr. Rodriguez said she had made her topic amusing.

"So what is it that you enjoy about your sister?"

"Well, she's bright and funny and quick to learn. And when she sets her mind on something she never gives up."

"I'll bet you know a few stories about her."

"Yes, but how do I choose which ones to include?"

"That's the tricky part, of course. Remember, this essay is a reflection of *you*. Try to choose stories that demonstrate how your sister has shaped the way you see the world. How old is your sister?"

"She's five."

"Just five years old and she is the one person you have chosen? I'm interested already. So, you "actually" enjoy her; she's not a pain with her whining or an annoying little shadow who is always tagging along?" asked Mr. Rodriguez.

"No," laughed Maddy.

"Why do you suppose that is?" asked Mr. Rodriguez.

"I never thought about it before," admitted Maddy.

"Well, think about it a little; it just might be the key to your essay."

"Okay," said Maddy already beginning to address the question in her mind.

Mr. Rodriguez was thoughtful for a moment before asking, "Maddy, the first time we went around the circle you mentioned your sister, but the second time you mentioned that you like to read fantasy stories. Were you thinking of a different topic the second time?"

"No, uh, I - I just couldn't think of anything else to say on the spot," she said feeling her face get hot.

"I see, not big on speaking in front of groups?"

"No, not really."

"That's okay, this is a writer's conference; we're not planning to tackle public speaking during this particular meeting," he smiled.

"That's good."

"After the break you will have a chance to begin working on your rough draft. We'll talk again after you've had some time to put some thoughts on paper. There will be three writing sessions so don't feel as though you need to get it down all at once. Writing is a process; it takes practice and a certain amount of patience. The ideas will come; they're already floating around in your head just waiting to be organized into your masterpiece."

Chapter 21

A Reflection of Yourself

MADDY AND MICHAEL WALKED out together. Alex was still talking with her coach and they didn't want to rush her. Michael was on the alert for any available snack and it didn't take him long to locate the crowd of students waiting to choose from a selection of ice cream bars. Maddy selected an orange creamsicle and Michael an ice cream sandwich.

"Guess this will have to hold me 'til dinner," said Michael between bites. "How's your topic coming along?"

"Okay, but I'll know better after I've had some time to work with it. How about you?"

"Same here," said Michael, "Hope I haven't bitten off more than I can chew."

"Interesting choice of words," noted Maddy.

"What?" asked Michael, his mouth full of ice cream sandwich.

"Very funny," said Maddy.

"No, I really mean it," insisted Michael, "I think I have a good topic, but I have to be careful not to say anything that will hurt my mom's feelings again."

"You'll manage it and it will be perfect," said Maddy.

"We'll see," said Michael doubtfully. "What about your topic?"

"I want to write about my sister, but I'm not sure yet what the focus will be. Mr. Rodriguez said to concentrate on how my relationship with Cassie has 'shaped the way I see the world'."

"Direct quote?"

"Yep."

"Actually, that's helpful advice since the paper is supposed to be a 'reflection of yourself'. You were lucky with your coach; I got an old lady who writes the society column for some small-town paper I never heard of. She's okay, but I think Mr. Daniels is at least as qualified to coach as she is."

"I don't see why you can't talk to Mr. Daniels, too. I'm sure he would have some good suggestions, especially since he knows your mom," offered Maddy.

Alex joined them just as Michael was licking the last sticky cookie crumbs off his fingers. "Where do we go next? I can't wait to get started," she enthused.

"Don't you want to get an ice cream first?" asked Michael.

"No, I think I'll just wait until dinner," she said, "Ice cream isn't a favorite of mine."

"Well geez, don't waste it, go pick up an ice cream sandwich and I'll eat it," said Michael.

"They won't let him have seconds?" Alex asked Maddy.

"Nope," said Maddy smiling.

"Oh alright, I'll get you one," she sighed and went over to the vendor. She returned with an ice cream cone covered with chopped nuts.

"I'm not big on nuts, but thanks," he said accepting the gift.

"Sorry, there wasn't a lot left to choose from. It was either that or a popsicle."

"You made the right choice."

"I thought as much," said Alex dryly, "So, does anyone know where we go next?"

"It doesn't say on the agenda," said Maddy consulting her sheet.

Miss Barber arrived, as if on cue, busily handing out room assignments. Maddy's said 214C, Alex had 212A and Michael was 215D. "Take the elevator to the second floor and exit to your left. Please do not exchange rooms, your coaches have been given this information and will stop in to check on your progress from time to time."

Maddy gave a small wave to Alex and Michael as she entered room 214. If she had been unimpressed earlier with the "materials provided", she wasn't anymore. This room was set up with four computer stations. There was a single printer for the room, and a water cooler. She took a seat in front of computer C and looked around the room. *Should I just start? Are there any instructions?*

She located the word processing program and opened it. She typed her sister's name: Mary Cassidy Schmidt

She was still staring at it when another student wandered in and found his place. She was staring at it when the last student arrived. There was a general nervous atmosphere in the room since this was new territory for the participants. At last Miss Barber bustled in with instruction sheets. Maddy began to read:

There will be three separate writing sessions at your computer station. Each student has been given a folder for saving his, or her, document(s). It is located on the computer desktop and will be labeled with your name. Please look for it to confirm that you are seated at the correct station.

To open the word processing program click on the blue "W" on the desktop. We suggest that you create three documents: a planning document, a rough draft and a final draft. Your final draft should be at least 500 words and no more than 1000 words in length.

If you have any technical questions about the use of the word processing program, saving or printing your work, please step into the hall to request assistance. Your coaches will stop in to see you at the end of the first session to check on your progress and offer assistance.

Good luck on your essay!

Maddy read the instruction sheet and searched the desktop for a folder with her name on it. She located it easily as it was separated from the other icons that lined the left side of the desktop. *How did I miss seeing it earlier?* She reopened her document and was once again faced with "Mary Cassidy Schmidt". She sighed. *Terrific, I'm stuck before I even get started!* She took a deep breath. *You can do this, just relax and think.*

She began to write. After a long while she had a few funny Cassie stories down on paper. She hoped she could piece them into something more coherent later. She tried to think about how Cassie had shaped her way of thinking about things, but couldn't come up with anything. *She's only five for heaven's sake! Do I have to admit to being influenced by a preschooler?* She checked the time: the first session was almost over! *I'll never be able to finish by tomorrow!* She was beginning to feel as though she had chosen a poor topic when Mr. Rodriguez came in to see her. Or maybe not, he was talking to 214A. Then she realized that he was mentoring all the students in the room. Mr. Rodriguez and 214A were sharing a laugh. *He won't be laughing when he sees what I have.*

At last Mr. Rodriguez made it to 214C.

"So, how are you doing?" he asked.

"Okay, I guess," said Maddy.

Mr. Rodriguez read what Maddy had so far. He chuckled a few times.

"Not bad," he said when he was finished, "she sounds like a real charmer."

"Thanks," said Maddy, encouraged, "I still need to figure out how she influences me."

"Don't over think it," suggested Mr. Rodriguez, "it's not as if she is someone you go to for advice. But I bet it's nice to see the world every so often from the uncomplicated perspective of a five-year-old, and you have a front row seat. Maybe you'll be able to share the view."

Maddy was beginning to see his point. She quickly reread what she had written looking at each memory from a new angle. "Thank you!" she told Mr. Rodriguez and she meant it. She was deep in thought as he moved on to the next student.

"Come on, Maddy, it's time for dinner!" It was Michael. "Save your work and let's go."

Maddy saved her paper to her folder but decided not to print anything. She really just needed to think; once she had the key she'd thought she'd be able to write it quickly enough.

Chapter 22

Leisure Time

MICHAEL GAVE DINNER two enthusiastic thumbs up. He had been delighted to see lasagna among the choices available. He had savored every morsel from the Caesar salad and garlic bread to the raspberry cheesecake. Maddy chose the Chicken Alfredo and Alex picked at the Pasta Primavera.

They spent much of their dinner conversation on their essays. Alex had completed her outline and some of the rough draft. She seemed to have a clear idea of what she hoped to accomplish with her piece. Maddy was impressed and a little jealous of her progress. Michael didn't say much about his essay except that he was glad to be able to use the computer instead of writing it out by hand. He was especially happy with the spell check function. Maddy offered that she was just starting to develop a thought prompted by Mr. Rodriguez's comments when she ran out of time. Eventually, the conversation ran to other topics.

"So," said Alex, "what are you planning to wear tomorrow night?"

"Clothes," replied Michael.

"I should hope so," returned Alex, who had quickly come to terms with Michael's flippant comments and lusty eating habits, "however, I was asking Maddy."

Maddy had forgotten all about her wardrobe problem.

"I don't know," she answered, "maybe after dinner we can go up and have a look in our room."

"But aren't you guys going to the 'Leisure activity'?" asked Michael.

"What is it?" asked Alex.

"Well, some of the kids are going to the pool and some are going to the movie showing in one of the conference rooms," said Michael.

"Do you have to choose one, or can you just go to your room?" asked Alex.

"Have to? It's leisure time, free time to have some fun! Don't you want to relax and enjoy yourself for a while?" asked Michael.

"I do," said Maddy immediately, "but I still need to figure out what I'm going to wear tomorrow. How about if I meet you at the pool by 7:15?"

"Good, I was hoping you'd choose the pool, I'll see you there. Are you going to finish that dessert?"

"No, you can have it," smiled Maddy.

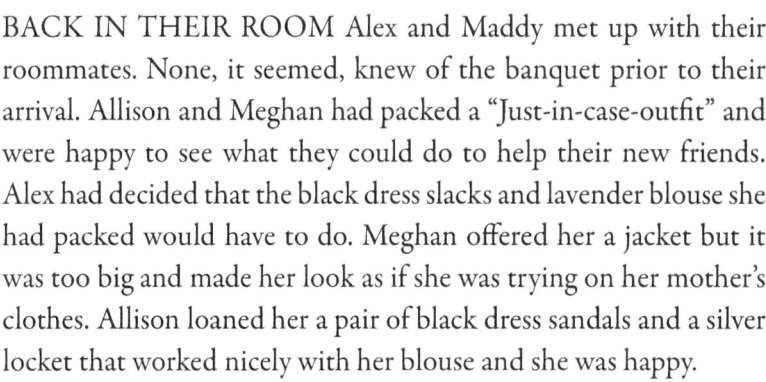

BACK IN THEIR ROOM Alex and Maddy met up with their roommates. None, it seemed, knew of the banquet prior to their arrival. Allison and Meghan had packed a "Just-in-case-outfit" and were happy to see what they could do to help their new friends. Alex had decided that the black dress slacks and lavender blouse she had packed would have to do. Meghan offered her a jacket but it was too big and made her look as if she was trying on her mother's clothes. Allison loaned her a pair of black dress sandals and a silver locket that worked nicely with her blouse and she was happy.

Maddy was having a more difficult time. She just didn't have anything dressy enough for a banquet. Jessica's pink beaded sweater was lovely, but she had nothing to go with it. Alex, Meghan and Allison went through their bags several times trying to find something suitable but without success. Finally, Allison saved the day by noticing the soft gray slacks that Meghan was wearing.

"They would look nice with the pink sweater, don't you think?" she asked.

"Of course! Why didn't we think of it sooner? I'll wash them out in the sink and we can iron them dry for Maddy to wear tomorrow night. She just needs to try them on to be sure they fit," insisted Meghan.

"This is so nice of you all, thanks so much," said Maddy gratefully.

She tried on the slacks with the sweater, which was a cardigan, buttoned all the way up. The delicate beadwork made jewelry unnecessary. She liked how the long smooth sleeves draped elegantly down her arms. Now that her problem was solved, she felt relieved and thought briefly about how much Jessica would enjoy hearing about how her sweater had saved the day. If only she had a camera; Jessica would love to see a picture.

Alex decided to stay in the room with Miss DePaula and work on her essay so Maddy headed down to the pool to meet Michael. She was only a few minutes late. Michael was easy to spot from his perch on the diving board. He had taken swimming and diving lessons since age four and was an accomplished swimmer and an even better diver. He was showing off a bit for the crowd doing somersaults and even an occasional splashy belly flop. In spite of his love for meals and snacks he had an athletic build. Maddy often wished she could eat the way he did and stay so trim.

He waved to her before diving with pinpoint precision into the pool and swam over to where she was wading carefully into the water from the steps.

"That's no way to enter a pool," he said critically.

"It's my way," Maddy declared stubbornly.

Maddy waded in until she was chest high and then floated on her back. Michael treaded water beside her.

"Sorry I'm a little late, but I did finally figure out what to wear tomorrow night. I'm going to borrow some slacks from Meghan and use the sweater Jessica gave me to wear."

"Jessie's gonna love that," said Michael.

"I had the same thought."

"Remind me to bring my phone, we'll get a picture," offered Michael.

"Have you figured out what to do with your paper yet?"

"Not exactly, but I did get a chance to talk to Mr. Daniels while I was waiting for you. I even told him the whole notebook story, which, by the way, he knows you know about. He suggested I might make my essay an apology of sorts emphasizing how she reacted to my objections in a positive way and how I wish things had happened differently. I've been thinking about it and I think I can make it work."

"I thought Mr. Daniels would be helpful," said Maddy.

"So how about your essay?" asked Michael.

"I'm still working out the bugs," admitted Maddy.

"I was really hoping you'd write about how you almost didn't get to come," said Michael.

"I can't believe I floated that idea into a room full of people! At least I came to my senses and realized that I might never leave my house ever again if my dad saw that published in the conference magazine. He'd probably ground me for life."

"Seems like you almost are already grounded for life," said Michael gently.

"Are you going to get on my case like Jessica now?" sighed Maddy.

"No," said Michael, "I just wish I could see you once in a while outside of school."

Maddy considered this. *What exactly does he mean by that?* She looked at him thoughtfully. "You mean like at the mall or movies or something?" she asked finally.

"Yeah, something like that," smiled Michael shyly. Then he abruptly swam off toward the diving board before she could see his face bloom scarlet.

Chapter 23

Finding the Key

━━━━●━━━━

MADDY, ALLISON AND Meghan returned to their room with no time to spare. They had remained at the pool until pointedly reminded by a scowling Mrs. Barber that leisure time ended *promptly* at 9:00 pm.

"Aren't you and Michael both from the same school?" asked Meghan coyly as they dripped down the hall.

"Yes," replied Maddy.

"He seems nice," she added, "how long have you known him?"

"Since third grade," answered Maddy.

"So, are you and Michael an item or what?" asked Allison who was tired of waiting for Meghan to get to the point.

"No, just good friends, I think," returned Maddy "what makes you think so?"

"Not much, he just paddled circles around you all night long and before you arrived, he only had eyes for the diving board," noted Allison.

"He did say something about wanting to see me outside of school for a movie or something, which was a first," said Maddy smiling at the thought.

"Meghan, we may have witnessed the actual first moments of a new relationship! I thought something was up between you two. What shoes are you planning to wear tomorrow night?"

"I only have the ones I'm wearing with me," she said indicating her feet with a shrug.

"We'll have to work on that," said Meghan, "We want you to look your best."

The trio returned to their room to find Alex bent over the desk working on her paper. She was sifting through several pages of handwritten notes and the waste basket was nearly full with her rejected ideas. She looked up when they came in.

"Back already?" she asked.

"It's after nine," Maddy replied, "Where's Miss DePaula?"

"She went to the vending machines for a snack, she should be right back."

"How's it going?" asked Maddy.

"Oh, pretty well, I think I'm almost finished."

"Really? But you have all day tomorrow still," said Allison, surprised.

"Well, I still need to type it into the computer and add the final touches," she replied.

"That won't take very long," commented Meghan.

"I'm not much of a typist," confessed Alex, adding, "I think better with pen and paper than a keyboard. I really needed time with my old-fashioned tools."

"You're just a throwback to a simpler time," smiled Maddy.

Alex smiled back grateful for the understanding.

"Well, we have some news and a small problem with shoes to work out before tomorrow night," said Allison changing the subject.

"Oh?" said Alex leaving a space for them to fill in with the news.

"Michael seems to have a thing for Maddy!" exclaimed Meghan.

"Of course he does, and I think it's mutual; I've been trying to stay out of their way all day," revealed Alex.

Maddy lay in bed thinking about her essay. Alex snored softly beside her and the room was quiet at last. Although she had enjoyed the giddy conversation with her new friends that began after "lights out" she was hoping for a little quiet time to plan out her essay. Like Alex needed time with paper and pen Maddy needed just some time to think on her own.

She relaxed into the soft pillows and thought about what she had written so far. She tried to re-imagine each anecdote thinking about why she had included it in the first place. *Why tell the story about Cassie and the great spaghetti struggle? Because it illustrates her stubborn persistence in the face of daunting challenges. And it was literally in her face, too!* She smiled remembering the orange cheeks that framed Cassie's mask of concentration. *I wish I could be more like that. I wish I could have her determination; I'd probably give up after a dropped noodle or two, but not Cassie. There was something else, too, what was it? She never really succeeded, but she never gave up either. Was it patience? Confidence? No, it was something more elusive. It was as though she never considered failure as something to get upset about.* Maddy thought about a baby just learning to walk. *He doesn't get embarrassed when he falls, he just gets up and tries again. Hmmm, that could be a useful quality to take into new situations.*

Maddy thought about Cassie's cleverness. She had included the "Brownilocks" story in her notes that afternoon, but was having second thoughts. It was an excellent example of how bright Cassie was and how quickly she could put new information to use, but somehow it just didn't seem to work. Including it would mean careful wording to be sure her mother didn't come off sounding impatient or resentful. She thought she would leave that kind of careful writing to Michael. There was something else, too. That particular story almost made her father seem tender and sweet and although she wouldn't negatively portray either of her parents, she was not inclined to make her father look good.

She was distracted for a while wondering how her father would react to the idea of his daughter going to a movie with Michael? She pushed the thought out of her mind and willed herself to concentrate on the more immediate problem of the essay. She remembered how Cassie had learned all the words to the theme song for *Gilligan's Island* at the ripe old age of two. She didn't really know what all the words meant and she had learned by the shear accident of having heard the song over and over during a Gilligan marathon on TV. She was so cute singing "a twee hour tooooor, a twee hour tooooor!"

What had Mr. Daniels said about Cassie? She will only be ten years old when I graduate high school. That was something to think about. She would have to go to a local school and live at home; she couldn't go away and leave her alone. Mr. Daniels might not think Cassie would need her big sister as much at age ten, but Maddy knew better. Again, she had to push the negative thoughts out of her mind.

Truth be known, she had latched on to Cassie as a topic out of desperation. She had listened to all the other students with their expensive hobbies: ballet, horseback riding and dog shows. Her only hobbies were reading and spending time with her family, especially Cassie. She did not aspire to anything so lofty as neurosurgery or piloting a plane. Her goals weren't set much higher than finishing 8th grade and getting into the magnet high school she had set her sights on.

She thought about Jessica and Michael's comments about her dad's restrictions on her outings. She hadn't thought to question his rules or, heaven forbid, challenge them. It was just the way things were. In a way, it forced her to be closer to her younger sister. She thought again about Mr. Rodriguez. *What had he said? He was impressed that the one person I would choose is a five-year-old. He wouldn't be so impressed if he knew how small my world is. He wondered if I ever consider her to be annoying or whiny, and of course she can be, but it doesn't really bother me most of the time. Why not?* That's when it came to her and Mr. Rodriguez was right: it was the key to her essay. That settled, she allowed drowsiness to assert itself more fully and easily drifted off to sleep with thoughts Michael floating at the edges of consciousness.

Chapter 24

Michael's Musings

MICHAEL LAY IN BED thinking about Maddy. In fact, he had been thinking about her a lot lately. He groaned remembering how he had clumsily hinted at a movie and had to swim away embarrassed. It had taken him three trips off the diving board before he had the nerve to swim back in her direction.

She didn't seem to notice, or, if she did she didn't seem to mind, though. He was beginning to realize how much he liked Maddy. He found her easy to talk with and he could say things to her he would never share with anyone else. Even so, he was surprised he told her about his brother. Still, he knew she would keep that private simply because he asked her to. He had never known her to pass along hurtful gossip unlike Jessie who just couldn't help herself.

He wondered, and not for the first time, about her father. He wondered if she would even be allowed to accept an invitation to the movies. *Was her dad just overprotective? Why doesn't her mom say anything? My mom sure would.* He remembered the adjective he had settled on to describe her dad: controlling. *Why would a grown man need to keep such tight control over a kid?* He made up his mind to see what his mom thought about it when he got home. He knew she was puzzled when Maddy met them at the car alone, with no parent to see her off. Maybe he could ask her about that as a way to start the conversation. It couldn't be any harder than that other conversation they'd had recently.

Meanwhile, he let his thoughts wander in a more pleasant direction and fell asleep imagining escorting Maddy to *Movies at the Mall.*

Chapter 25

The Patterson Presentation

MADDY WOKE UP FIRST and padded quietly into the bathroom to brush her teeth and get dressed. The alarm clock was just beginning to ring as she came out and she decided not to shut it off, but let one of the remaining sleepers see to it. She thought it was fair to allow the bathroom to be awarded on a first come, first served basis and she waited to see who that might be. It was Alex, she noted with a certain amount of satisfaction. Miss DePaula was starting to stir as well. She gave her a moment or two to clear her head before letting her know that she was heading down to breakfast.

The hotel restaurant was just beginning to show signs of life as servers carried out steaming trays of scrambled eggs, bacon, and grits to the warming bins. The coffee stations offered decaf, a mild breakfast roast and a "robust" offering for the especially sleepy. Tea, milk, and several juice selections were available at one end of the mock kitchen set-up. The other end provided a waffle iron with pre-measured batter, a toaster with bread and English muffins and an assortment of breakfast pastries. They even had a selection of those little cereal boxes. Maddy smiled thinking how happy Michael would be when he saw it.

She was seated with juice, scrambled eggs, and the weekend edition of USA Today when Michael arrived. It did not take him long to overwhelm his Styrofoam plate with food and place it next to Maddy with a flourish. He then returned to the buffet to collect a coffee mug filled with orange juice and a small plate loaded with tiny muffins and a cheese Danish.

"My favorite: an all-you-can-eat buffet!" he said with evident enthusiasm.

Maddy smiled and shook her head.

"So did you sleep on it and figure out what to do with your essay?" he asked.

"As a matter of fact, I think I did," said Maddy happily.

"Any chance you'll finish early? I heard a rumor that you can have 'leisure time' once you turn in your final draft this afternoon," he informed her.

"Really? Wow, Alex is going to have a lot of time on her hands. I think she pretty much finished her essay last night in our room. She says all she has to do is type up the final draft and polish a bit," said Maddy.

Now it was Michael's turn to shake his head. "Yeah, but she missed out on 'leisure time'," he insisted, "and 'leisure time' is very important."

"You're really enjoying saying 'leisure time' aren't you?" said Maddy.

"Very much so," said Michael.

"She said she was more comfortable working it out with pen and paper. I don't think she cares for the computers so much," explained Maddy.

"Well, I don't see why she didn't just use paper and pen instead then. I don't think anyone is forcing her to use the computer, are they?" he asked.

Maddy considered this a typical Michael observation. "Not everyone is as comfortable in the role of nonconformist, Michael," she pointed out adding, "She probably assumed she had to use them; I did."

"She could have asked someone," he returned.

"Again, not everyone is as comfortable talking to adults as you are," she countered.

"They're just people for Pete's sake; the worst thing that could happen is they say that they are very sorry, but she will have to rough it with modern technology," he argued.

"Maybe she's a little shy with adults," Maddy supposed.

"Maybe," allowed Michael, "It just seems to me that most of the adults around here genuinely seem to want to help. This was supposed to be a sort of treat after all. I don't think anyone wants us to fail."

"Alex takes it all very seriously, maybe she puts pressure on herself," said Maddy.

"Speak of the devil," said Michael as Alex arrived. She selected a box of Cheerios and a glass of milk before slumping next to Maddy at the table.

"Not a morning person, eh?" noted Michael.

Alex grunted.

"Good news!" he tried again, "Did you know that you get free time as soon as you turn in your final draft? I heard you got a lot done last night."

Alex mumbled something unintelligible. Maddy and Michael exchanged looks.

"Is this normal morning behavior for you, Alex?" asked Maddy.

Alex nodded, "Except I'm usually not dressed by now."

"Ah, your first complete sentence, congratulations!" said Michael a little too heartily.

BY THE TIME THEY WERE settled in their seats in Conference Room C Alex had rallied. Soon Miss Barber arrived to introduce the morning's speaker, Mrs. Cynthia Patterson. She described the wide variety of careers in the writing field. Her discussion was lively and entertaining. She seemed to a have a funny story for every potential career option from proofreaders and editors to journalists and novelists. The group leaving this presentation, although composed of the same individuals, was far more animated and excited than the previous morning's attendees.

"They should have had her speak yesterday, instead of Mr. Excitement," said Michael as they made their way to the elevators.

"Guess they wanted to save the best for last," offered Alex.

"Of the two, she was the better motivator, so I'd have used her first to get everyone enthused about their writing," said Maddy.

"I had never really thought about a career in writing before; it seemed sort of boring, just sitting around a computer screen all day. I guess it doesn't have to be that way," said Michael.

"I guess not, reporters have to get out and get the story after all. They can't just make up the news sitting at their computers. And sometimes they get to interview famous people, that would be cool," said Alex.

"I think I'd like to be a sports writer. I can see myself in the press box at Yankee Stadium," fantasized Michael, "then, after the game I'd get to interview players in the locker room. And I bet they don't even have to pay for tickets!"

"Of course, you'd have to work your way up from little league games, like the guy Ms Patterson told us about," pointed out Maddy.

"There are always dues to pay, I guess," chuckled Michael as he recalled the story in which the unsuspecting umpire turned to find a seven-year-old's frustrated father on the wrong side of the fence and armed with such unlikely weapons as an eye chart and a chili dog.

"Of course, I'm sure you'd put in your time on the smaller stuff, and work your way up to the more interesting assignments. You're definitely a 'go-getter'" assured Maddy.

"So, what about you, Maddy? Is there a writing career that appeals to you?" asked Alex.

"I think it would be fun to write fiction. I like the idea of creating characters and a whole little world for them to explore," mused Maddy.

"What kind of world would you create?" asked Michael.

"I'm not sure, I'd have to give it some thought," replied Maddy "and right now I need to focus on my essay."

"Well, here's your chance," said Michael as they reached Maddy's work station, "I'll see you at lunch."

"See you later," said Alex.

Chapter 26

Feedback

THE ONLY SOUND IN THE room was the gentle tapping of computer keys as the students worked on their essays. Everyone seemed focused on their work. All the restlessness and hesitancy of the previous day was gone as the students worked toward their deadline.

Maddy worked quickly and thoughtfully. She had made adjustments to her planning document and printed it out to serve as a sort of road map for her paper. She consulted it from time to time as she hammered out her rough draft. She was pleased with her progress; the writing had gone quickly as she had expected it would once she had a clear idea of what she wanted to accomplish. She had completed the rough draft and saved it. Then she cut and pasted the rough draft into a whole new document which would become her final draft after some additional work.

She was working on the final draft when Mr. Rodriguez came in to check on her. He was happy to hear that she had a finished rough draft. She printed it out so he could make notations on it and continued her work on the final draft while he read through her piece.

"This is very nice work, Maddy," he told her returning her draft. "I like the fact that you created a planning document and rough draft as suggested, not many people did. You'll be able to see how your piece has evolved by reviewing your revisions. How's your final version coming? It looks like you're about finished."

"Oh, no I'm not even close. I just copied the rough draft to work from. That's okay isn't it?"

"Sure, that was a good idea. It'll save you typing, but you'll still be able to see the difference between your two drafts. I look forward to seeing the finished product." Mr. Rodriguez moved on to the next student.

Maddy looked at the pages Mr. Rodriguez had returned to her. There were no notations or comments on it anywhere. Maddy was surprised. He hadn't really given her any feedback about the content of her essay. He only seemed impressed that she could follow directions. She picked up the instruction sheet from the previous day: We suggest that you create three documents: a planning document, a rough draft and a final draft.

"We suggest". *So it was only a suggestion. Well, how about that!* She wondered if she would have created all three documents if she had been aware that it was optional. She had just assumed that the instructions were, "the rules", after all they were handed out by Miss Barber, a rule follower if there ever was one.

A few moments later Alex arrived to see if she was ready to go to lunch. Maddy was surprised that she had arrived before Michael, but then she remembered that Alex had all but completed her essay the previous evening. Still, it wasn't at all like Michael to be late for a meal. Alex noticed it, too.

"Where's Michael? I heard that we're having Mexican food for lunch. How does he like tacos, burritos and quesadillas?" she asked.

"If it's food, he probably likes it," replied Maddy, "but I wonder what's keeping him."

"Maybe he's still waiting to talk to his mentor," guessed Alex, "What room is he in?"

"He was 215D I think," said Maddy.

"You remember the exact station?" asked Alex raising an eyebrow.

Maddy ignored this. They walked together down the hall toward room 215. Michael was there and so was his mentor. They were deep in concentration and Maddy noticed that Michael seemed to be doing his best to keep a lid on his frustration. His mouth was fixed in a tight straight line as though he was afraid of what might escape if he relaxed. His right knee bounced quickly up and down as though eager to be on its way.

"Maybe we should wait for him," said Alex.

"No, I think we should go on ahead. He'll know where to find us," decided Maddy.

Maddy and Alex were laughing over two very messy tacos when Michael finally arrived. He was carrying a tray laden with nachos and quesadillas. Maddy thought it a minor miracle that his plate could bear the load. Alex's eyes were wide with wonder as he placed his plate on the table and immediately headed back toward the buffet.

"Where are you going?" she asked incredulously.

"I need something to drink," replied Michael as if it should be obvious.

"Oh," said Alex, "of course."

Michael returned with a large soda. "Lord have mercy! I thought she'd never let me leave. I'm starved!" he exclaimed as he settled in to enjoy his lunch.

"So, how's your essay coming?" asked Maddy.

"Well, the content is "absolutely delightful", but evidently my grammar and spelling are atrocious," said Michael between bites.

"Didn't you use the spell check?" asked Alex.

"Of course I did, but it doesn't help if the word is 'spelled correctly, but used inappropriately'". The last half of this sentence was spoken in Michael's best old lady imitation.

"What?" asked Alex, confused.

Michael continued to mimic his mentor. "Well dear, it seems you have used the possessive, *their* instead of the adverb *there*, as in here and there, which you intend. And over here, sweetie, you need to remove the apostrophe from it's even though it is the possessive form. The possessive of the word, it, is the exception to the rule when it comes to the use of the apostrophe." Here he dropped the old lady bit. "I'm losing my mind!! I wish she'd just circle my mistakes in red pen and leave out all the lengthy explanations. I'll never finish at this rate."

"*There, there* dearie *it's* going to be alright," soothed Maddy in an old lady voice of her own.

Alex couldn't resist joining in. "As you can see," she said in her best instructor voice, "Maddy has used the interjection, there, spelled the same as the adverb form, and followed it with the contraction of 'it is' where the apostrophe signifies the missing letter."

"Very funny," said Michael, "now, can we talk about something else? How are your essays?"

"Mine is coming along nicely," volunteered Alex, "I'm still typing up the final draft."

"I thought you'd be finished by now," said Michael.

"Nope, I'm still typing and fine tuning," said Alex.

"What did your mentor tell you?" asked Maddy.

"She said she liked the opening where I talk about a recent visit to see Nana at the nursing home. She said it was a nice idea to open with the present before talking about the days before her illnesses became so serious. She said it makes the story "less linear" and that it folds together nicely when I return to my recent visit at the end of the piece."

"Wow, sounds like you nailed it," said Michael.

"Yeah, and you got real feedback about your content. All I got was a pat on the back for creating an outline and rough draft as *suggested,*" said Maddy sulking.

"Maybe he didn't need to say anything because the content was good," offered Michael.

"I can't believe he didn't say anything," said Alex.

"He just said it was 'nice work' and then went on and on about how I'll be able to contrast my earlier draft with the final draft. I was hoping to hear something about my topic or writing style or something besides good for you for following directions!" complained Maddy.

"Did you make a rough draft separate from your final draft?" Michael asked Alex.

"Sort of, but I worked it out with pen and paper last night instead of on the computer and I threw the outline away after I finished the first draft. Did you?" asked Alex.

"Nope," said Michael, unconcerned.

"Does it matter?" asked Alex.

"No, I'm sure it's fine," snapped Maddy. "I'm probably the only one who thought that I had to follow the directions to the letter."

Michael was beginning to notice that Maddy was really bothered. He couldn't decide what was bothering her more. Although she said she just wanted to hear something about her writing, she really seemed to be upset with herself and he couldn't make out why that should be.

"I'd be happy to trade coaches with you, just say the word," offered Michael.

"Thanks, but no thanks," smiled Maddy, "I guess I just wanted to hear something more concrete about my work. I thought he'd say something specific. I hope I'm on the right track," she explained.

"Is there a wrong track? I'm surprised that you're worried, remember we're all just here to improve our skills and do our best. Anyway, that's what my old lady mentor told me," said Michael.

"Don't you even know her name?" asked Alex.

"Yes, I do, but I prefer "old lady mentor" to Mrs. Mildred Murphree."

Alex and Maddy giggled.

Chapter 27

More Feedback

———————○———————

MICHAEL WAS THE VERY first student to turn in his completed essay at exactly 3:00. He quietly paced the small stretch of hallway between rooms 212 and 214 waiting for Alex or Maddy to finish. He was in a good mood: the work was over and the rest of the conference was all about food and "leisure time".

After a few minutes Miss Barber asked him to leave the hallway and wait elsewhere. She was afraid other students might begin to rush their work if they saw him "loitering in the halls". Michael nodded and walked slowly toward the end of the hall where the elevators were located. He pushed the "up" button intending to go to the topmost floor to check out the view. The elevator doors slid open and Mr. Daniels exited.

"Hello, Michael, finished already?" he asked.

The elevator doors closed smoothly.

"Yep," he replied happy to see a friendly face, "I'm just waiting for Maddy."

"You could have fooled me, I thought you were waiting for the elevator," replied Mr. Daniels.

"Oh, very funny," said Michael dryly, "well, I was told not to loiter in the halls so I was leaving the floor." He did his best not to sound sulky.

"I see," said Mr. Daniels, "so where is Miss Barber anyway?"

"She's just down the -—hey Mr. D. how did you know-?"

Mr. Daniels winked and headed down the hall. Michael watched him walk away and was happy to see a few more students emerging from their rooms. There was still no sign of Maddy or Alex, but he decided to remain with the group who were also loitering in the hallway. A few students were whispering together when Miss Barber strode up followed by Mr. Daniels.

"You students may not remain in the hall while others are still writing!!" she hissed, adding, "Young man I am sure I have already spoken to you once about this!"

"But ma'am, where do we go? Do we just go back to our rooms or can we go to the lobby?" asked one bold young lady.

"Ah, I think I see the problem," Mr. Daniels interceded, "we neglected to be specific about where the students are permitted to go if they finish early. May I suggest that these students accompany me to the lobby area and request that a few other chaperones join us there since the group is likely to grow larger?"

"Yes, thank you Mr. Daniels," said Miss Barber, "that is an excellent idea."

The group headed for the main staircase that descended one level to the lobby.

"Thanks, Mr. D.," said Michael.

"No problem," returned Mr. Daniels, "so are you happy with your essay?"

"Sure," said Michael, "it wasn't too bad once I got going. My coach was a little annoying though."

"Annoying?"

"Yeah, she didn't just point out my mistakes, she lectured me on them making sure I understood why each and every single change was required."

"Good for her, I hope you learned something."

"Don't turn into the enemy Mr. D."

"Why Michael, surely you don't consider teachers to be enemies?"

"She's not a teacher, she a columnist for some dinky paper I never heard of and let's just say she made the learning process painful."

"Teachers aren't just school employees with certificates. There are lots of teachers in your life. The important question to answer is: Did learning occur?"

"Well, I can definitely say that I will never again confuse the words: T-H-E-R-E,

T-H-E-I-R,   and   T-H-E-Y-apostrophe-R-E!"   admitted Michael.

"Excellent!" enthused Mr. Daniels. Michael rolled his eyes.

Maddy joined the lobby group just after 3:30.

"Wow, I expected Alex to finish before you; I wonder what's keeping her?" asked Michael.

"She isn't out yet?" asked Maddy.

"Why should she be done so quickly, if you don't mind my asking," interjected Mr. Daniels.

"Well, she stayed in all night last night working on it, that's all," answered Michael. Maddy shot him a look. Michael shrugged and looked puzzled by her reaction.

"I see," said Mr. Daniels "she's probably just putting on the final touches. So, Maddy, are you happy with your essay?"

"I think so, uh, I made a copy before I left the room. Was that okay?" she asked.

"I don't see why not," said Mr. Daniels.

"I wish I'd thought of that," complained Michael, "Can I read it?"

"Well, I'm not sure we're supposed to..." began Maddy.

"Eventually everyone will read it since it will be published," observed Mr. Daniels.

"I guess."

"I know, why don't you read it Mr. D.? After all, you're her Language Arts teacher," suggested Michael. Maddy shot him a second warning look.

"I would be delighted to read it," smiled Mr. Daniels.

Maddy handed him her copy with a nervous smile. She and Michael walked a short distance away to give him a moment to read it.

"Michael, why did you do that?" she hissed.

"Why not? It's not a state secret, is it? And you did want some feedback as I recall," Michael defended himself.

"Well, it's too late for feedback now that I've finished it!" she returned.

"It will be fine, you'll see," Michael assured her, "By the way, what was that look you gave me when I was talking to Mr. D. about Alex?"

"I just don't think Alex would want you to point out how hard she's worked on her paper, that's all."

"Since when is working hard a bad thing?" asked Michael.

"It's not, but, oh, I can't explain it right. I just think she's a sort of private person and might not like everyone to know every little thing about her writing process," Maddy said frustrated at Michael for being so typically Michael.

"You mean she wouldn't want everyone to know that she needed extra time?"

"Maybe, or maybe that she prefers pen and paper to keyboard and screen."

They ended their discussion when they noticed that Mr. Daniels was rejoining them.

"So, how is it, Mr. D.?" asked Michael.

"It's quite good. Maddy, you do a nice job describing a very charming young lady and by the end of the piece I felt all of your concern for her. I was especially struck by the phrase where you worry over 'more than her safety'. That was a very interesting way to talk about the loss of innocence that happens to everyone at some point." Mr. Daniels returned her paper to her and added, "I'm so glad you were able to attend this workshop."

"Thank you," said Maddy as she took the paper. She was blushing furiously and

appeared to have developed a sudden fascination for her feet. Mr. Daniels patted her shoulder and walked back toward the group which by this time was getting larger with no other chaperones in sight.

"May I read it?" asked Michael almost shyly.

"I guess," said Maddy. She sat on the edge of a planter and waited for him to read through her paper.

He stopped at one point to ask, "She never did succeed with the spaghetti?"

"Oh, maybe a noodle or two, but not much more," smiled Maddy.

"Poor baby," replied Michael.

"Better not let her hear you call her that," warned Maddy.

Michael pretended to look nervously over his shoulder. "Good thing she's not here then," he said. He continued to read. When he finished he looked thoughtful but didn't say anything for a while. Maddy was quiet, too.

After a few minutes he asked, "Maddy, who did you trust that let you down?"

Chapter 28

Technical Difficulties

ALEX WAS THE VERY LAST student to turn in her paper at 5:09. She had no problem writing her essay, but her typing skills were nonexistent and she had spent the day hunting and pecking and correcting. Finally, at the end of the first session she had closed her paper without saving her work. She did not realize that anything was wrong until the afternoon session had begun and she didn't find her essay in her labeled folder. *How could I make such a stupid mistake?* She remembered that the prompt had come up: Do you want to save your changes? *I know I clicked on* "YES". *Even I know enough about computers to save my work.* Well, there was no use crying about it. She repeated the tedious hunting and pecking and correcting process. When her mentor came in she explained her problems and she only added to her frustration by locating her morning's work! She had saved her work, but not to her folder. Instead, she had saved it to the hard drive of the computer where her mentor had found it by searching all documents.

Although she was tempted to scream in frustration her more practical side took over. Now she had to decide whether to use the morning's version or continue the afternoon's work. Which would be easier? She had already edited so much that they were very different pieces. After rereading both papers she decided to continue working on the afternoon version. There would be too many revisions and too little time to edit the morning's draft. She checked her time and knew she could finish typing it in and then read through it to check for errors. Each time one of her fellow students left she felt more pressure. By 4:30 she had the room to herself. There were so many typos! At 5:00 one of the coaches came in to see if she was ready. He told her she could continue working while he printed out the papers from the other three stations and collected their work on a disc. At last he could wait no longer.

"Sorry, but we're out of time," he said gently.

"Okay, I think it's as good as it's going to get," she replied, "thanks for the extra few minutes."

"Why didn't you ask for help?" he asked.

"I didn't know that anything was wrong until after lunch, and then, I didn't realize that there was anything that could be done," she answered ruefully.

"Well, I have to say that I'm impressed that you hung in there; I've seen participants in tears over much smaller setbacks," he said.

"Oh, I considered a good cry for a while there," she admitted.

"Would you like a hard copy to take with you?" he asked.

"Yes, please!"

Alex walked into the empty hall and headed for the elevator. She thought she would check at the pool for Maddy and Michael since they had enjoyed it the day before. Instead, she decided to check out the view from the top floor; she hadn't been up there yet and wanted to take a look around.

The view was interesting. She could see the largest features of some of the area theme parks off in the distance. She wondered if there might be fireworks later in the evening since they often end the day at the big parks with a spectacular light show or fireworks finale of some sort. She made a mental note to suggest it to Maddy and Michael; it might make a nice ending to the banquet as long as they weren't late getting to their rooms for lights out.

After a few minutes she got back on the elevator and pushed the button labeled, lobby. On the eighth floor two of the conference mentors boarded the elevator. They were discussing the decision to choose the top three essays for mention at the banquet that evening. Those would be the same ones that would be published in the paper. It had been a difficult choice because they had gotten a good crop of essays out of this group. *They always say that* thought Alex to herself wondering if they just said it because she was in the elevator with them.

Everyone exited at the lobby and Alex headed in the direction of the pool but was careful to stay behind the two mentors as long as they continued in her direction.

"I particularly liked the Schmidt girl's piece," said one.

"Yes, I intend to rank it first," said the other.

"She shows a lot of insight for someone so young," said the first.

"Loss of innocence," mused the other, "such a mature theme."

Alex reached the hallway that led to the pool area. She was tempted to continue following the pair of mentors, but decided against it. At the pool she quickly located Maddy and Michael and made her way to them.

"Hi!" said Maddy when she saw her approach.

"Where's your swim suit?" asked Michael.

"I wasn't sure where I'd find you so I didn't go back to my room. I just finished my essay," she replied.

"You just finished?" asked Michael.

"It's a long story and not very interesting so I'll spare you the details. Let's just say I experienced some technical difficulties," said Alex.

"Sorry to hear it," said Michael, "Are you going to swim?"

"I don't think so, it's too much trouble to go up and change, then change again later for the banquet. I think I'll just skip it."

"What time is it?" asked Maddy.

"About 5:30," replied Alex, "Did you ever solve your shoe problem?"

"Nah, but that's okay. I'll just wear my flats. I don't think anyone will notice since we'll be seated at the table most of the evening," replied Maddy.

"I overheard an interesting conversation in the elevator on my way down," began Alex.

"Eavesdropping Alex? It doesn't become you," said Michael.

"We were in an elevator, Michael," objected Alex although she neglected to mention following them after they arrived on the first floor.

"Who were you with?" asked Maddy.

"Two mentors from the conference and they were talking about ranking their favorite essays. There was one in particular they liked very much for its "mature theme". They said it was insightful," related Alex.

"Did they say who wrote it?" asked Michael.

"They did, but they used the last name and I didn't recognize it," replied Alex, "Darn, I can't remember it now. Give me a few minutes and I'll think of it."

"It wasn't Evans was it?" asked Michael with a twinkle in his eye.

"No, I think it was a girl's essay. Of course, it couldn't have been mine since I took so long to finish no one could have read it yet," said Alex.

"I guess we'll find out soon enough," said Maddy, "Is that your essay?" She indicated the folded pages in Alex's fingertips.

"Yeah, want to read it?" she offered.

"Sure," said Maddy climbing out of the pool and grabbing a towel.

"Man," complained Michael, "am I the only one who didn't print a copy?"

Chapter 29

Sarah Who?

MEGHAN AND ALLISON were waiting expectantly for Maddy's arrival. They had something behind their backs and looked exceptionally pleased with themselves.

"Hi," said Maddy a little surprised to be greeted at the door. Alex had arrived a few minutes ahead of Maddy; she was flipping through a magazine in a chair near the windows. She looked up and nodded a greeting.

"Hi, yourself," said Meghan, "it's about time you got here. You need to get ready for the banquet."

"We have something for you," said Allison.

"I just hope they fit," worried Meghan as she brought out a pair of silver sandals.

"Wow, they're gorgeous!" enthused Maddy, "where did you get them?"

"Well, it wasn't easy. We asked just about every girl here but no one had anything we could use," said Meghan.

"They really should have let us know about this banquet in the materials we received. I'm going to complain to someone about it," said Allison importantly.

"But where did you get them?" asked Maddy again.

"I bought them downstairs in one of the shops!" said Meghan triumphantly.

"You *bought* them?" Maddy could not believe her ears.

"Sure, try them on, I bought them in my size. I'm just letting you borrow them from me, that is, if they fit."

Maddy slid her foot into them easily. "I feel like Cinderella," she laughed.

"Okay," said Allison taking charge, "Go take a shower, and be sure to wash your hair thoroughly and use the conditioner. The chlorine in that pool you're so fond of isn't doing nice things for your hair!"

"You only have about fifteen minutes for your shower. Then we get you for hair and makeup!" said Meghan.

By 7:20 Allison and Meghan were putting the finishing touches on their project. Maddy went along for the most part allowing them to be creative with her hair. She was worried they might go overboard with her makeup but her only objection was to refuse the mascara Allison wanted to use.

Michael arrived a few minutes later.

"You look terrific," he told Maddy and promptly asked Alex to snap a picture of them together. Next, he took a shot of Maddy and Alex and then one of the four roommates together. "If you guys give me your phone numbers, I'll text you copies of these and whatever I take at the banquet," he offered.

They arrived in the ballroom to find tables lavishly set with a Caesar salad waiting at each place. Michael was concerned to see that the seats were assigned until he saw that students from the same school were kept together. He was relieved to see that Allison, Meghan, and Alex were not assigned to their table. He didn't know them very well and they seemed nice, they certainly had been generous to Maddy, still, they made him feel a little self-conscious.

After a few opening remarks from Miss Barber and introductions of the dignitaries seated at the head table the guests were invited to begin dining. Waiters came to take drink orders and leave a short menu from which they could choose an entrée. Michael suggested the chicken cordon bleu.

"What could be better?" he asked, "it's got everything: chicken stuffed with ham and swiss. Meat, meat and cheese!"

Maddy smiled, "It sounds good, but I think I'll try the stuffed salmon."

"That sounds good, too," he agreed, "I wish I could order both."

"You can taste some of mine if you want," offered Maddy.

"That's a good idea, you can try some of my chicken, too," enthused Michael.

After the waiters took their orders, Michael brought out a crumpled sheet of paper.

"What's that?" asked Maddy.

"I finally found someone to print a copy of my essay, want to read it?" replied Michael.

"Oh, yes!" said Maddy taking it from him. She read through the page aware of Michael's knee bouncing nervously beside her while she read. When she was finished, she looked at him admiringly.

"Michael you are the only person I know who can call his mother a liar and mean it as a compliment! This is so good, it's funny and straightforward just like you are. I wish I could write with humor the way you do," she said at last.

"Thanks, I wish I had let you read it sooner. I kept worrying that I might hurt her feelings again if I said things wrong," admitted Michael.

"I think you made her sound wonderful," said Maddy.

The meal concluded with a dessert of chocolate cake which met with Michael's enthusiastic approval. At last Miss Barber stood and approached the microphone.

"Well, I certainly hope you have enjoyed the conference. We have been particularly pleased with the work of this year's participants. As you know all the essays will be published in a magazine format which we hope to have available the first week of January. In addition, we would like to acknowledge a few essays this evening as especially thought-provoking. As I said, all of this year's participants were excellent and it has been very hard to choose the three best pieces. As a matter of fact, final decisions about the three to be published in the Times have not been made at this time. We have narrowed our selection down to ten finalists who will be named this evening. These ten finalists will receive a trophy like this one as soon as they can be engraved." She held aloft a trophy in the shape of an open book. She continued, "Students, please come forward if your name is called to receive a certificate of achievement."

"Joseph Canales ... Tameka Connolly ... Michael Evans...." Michael jumped up and pumped his fist into the air when his name was called. He bounded to the stage to shake hands with the people seated at the head table. Miss Barber handed him his certificate.

Maddy was happy for him and applauded as he rejoined the table. "Jessica Jones... Marques Mackey... Bryan Perkins... Michelle Rodriguez... Sarah Schmidt... Jennifer Tomlinson... Thomas Wright."

It took a few moments for Maddy and Michael to notice the confusion at the head table. They saw Mr. Daniels rise and whisper to Miss Barber who seemed somewhat flustered. After a moment Miss Barber returned to the microphone.

"It seems that we have one certificate remaining for a Sarah Schmidt but I have just been informed that she is accustomed to being called, Maddy. Maddy Schmidt, will you please come up for your award?"

Maddy was mortified. She hadn't even recognized her own name! She had been listening for Alex's name to be called. Alex had worked so hard on her paper. Maddy was sure she would be called forward. Michael gave her a gentle shove toward the front of the room, "Go on; don't keep everyone waiting."

Maddy accepted her congratulations and her certificate and returned to her seat scanning the room for Alex. She spotted her sitting near the back of the room. She was relieved to see that she didn't look terribly disappointed; in fact, she was smiling and waving at her.

The festivities ended soon after the presentations. Alex made her way toward Michael and Maddy through the crowd.

"Congratulations guys!" she said.

"Thanks!" said Michael and Maddy together.

"Want to go up to the top floor and watch some fireworks?" suggested Alex.

"Oh, that's a great idea," said Michael.

"Fireworks?" asked Maddy.

"Come on, we'll show you," said Alex and Michael together.

Chapter 30

After Dinner Conversations

THEY WEREN'T THE ONLY ones checking out the view from the top floor. A small group had gathered to check out the fireworks display. After a few minutes Alex whispered something to Michael who nodded. Michael walked over to Maddy, took her hand and led her to the stairwell where they went down one floor.

"The view is just as good from here, but there's no crowd," said Michael.

"But we left Alex alone," objected Maddy who was slightly distracted by the fact that Michael was still holding her hand.

"It was her suggestion," returned Michael.

They sat on the carpet and watched the fireworks through the large floor to ceiling windows.

"This is so cool," said Maddy.

"Yeah," agreed Michael.

"I managed to get a picture of you accepting your certificate," said Michael.

"You did? I wish I had thought to do that for you," fretted Maddy.

"You couldn't have anyway, I had my phone with me," said Michael.

"I felt so stupid not recognizing my own name," said Maddy.

"I'm not used to hearing you called Sarah, I like Maddy much better," said Michael helpfully.

"I was actually listening for Alex's name, did you read her essay? It was good," insisted Maddy.

"I didn't read it. I only read yours which was excellent. I can't believe I didn't react to your name being read out because I was absolutely sure it would be called. I'd be surprised if you weren't one of the three published," he said.

"Well, thanks, but neither of us has had a chance to read any of the other essays so who is to say that it's the best?" asked Maddy.

"Well, it was a step above mine."

"I don't think so, yours was funny."

"Yours was serious and a little sad. You know, you never answered my question earlier."

"I know, I don't think I want to talk about that."

"Okay."

"I wish tonight could last a little longer."

"Me, too."

Michael returned Maddy to her room at precisely 9:30. Maddy was afraid he'd get caught in the halls by the ever-vigilant Miss Barber. Michael, who had already been cornered by Miss Barber once that day, was also hoping to avoid a second encounter.

"Well, I hate to kiss and run. I had a great time tonight, see you in the morning," he blurted just before giving her a quick kiss and dashing off.

"Good night," Maddy called after him.

Allison, Meghan and Alex were waiting, already changed into pajamas when Maddy returned.

"So, how was it?" asked Meghan.

"It was great. Thanks for loaning me the slacks and the sandals Meghan, that was incredibly nice of you," said Maddy.

"It was nothing, I'm glad we can wear the same size," said Meghan.

"And thanks to both of you for the help with my hair and makeup, I'm totally clueless about that stuff," said Maddy.

"No problem," Allison replied, then added with a grin, "You missed your own name being called out! That was hilarious!"

"I know," said Maddy, "I'm not used to being called Sarah."

"I love the name, Sarah," said Alex, "it's much better than having a guy's name."

"Oh, I really like your name," insisted Maddy, "it's unique for a girl to have such a strong sounding name."

"Strong? It makes me think of a nearsighted accountant," objected Alex.

"That's interesting, it makes me think of Alexander the Great," observed Maddy.

"Really? I'll have to remember that," said Alex thoughtfully.

"I guess congratulations are in order," said Meghan.

"Yeah, both you and Michael were recognized," added Allison.

"Speaking of Michael, did you two have fun tonight?" asked Meghan, "Alex told us you went up to the top floor to watch the fireworks."

"Yes, but we didn't have much time before we had to be back in our rooms," replied Maddy.

"Oooh, that's a good sign," observed Meghan.

"They didn't want the evening to end," said Allison wistfully.

Alex just smiled and shook her head.

"Of course, the big question of the night is: did he kiss you?" asked Meghan.

Alex's eyes widened in surprise, "Meghan, that's personal!" she sputtered.

"But don't you want to know?" asked Allison incredulously.

"Well ..." Alex stammered, "if she wants us to know she'll say something on her own."

"She hasn't told us yet and we're running out of time," returned Allison.

Alex's objection had given Maddy an extra moment to consider her reply. Normally she wouldn't share anything so personal, but the events of the conference hadn't been anything like her normal day to day life. It occurred to her that she would miss these new friends. It also occurred to her that they would be returning to their own schools and it was unlikely that they could pass on gossip to anyone in her circle.

"We held hands a little while we watched the fireworks and he kissed me at the door," she revealed.

"He did? That's wonderful!" exclaimed Meghan.

"I knew it!" said Allison.

They were interrupted by a knock on the door. "Lights out!" called Miss Barber.

Chapter 31

Lights Out

———○———

ALEX AND MADDY STAYED up well past lights out discussing the events of the day. They promised to keep in touch and eventually came to realize that they were both hoping to enter the same magnet high school program.

"We could see each other in high school!" said Maddy.

"That's two years away," pointed out Alex.

They each promised to do everything they could to be accepted into the college preparatory program they were applying to.

"Is Michael applying to the same school?" asked Alex.

"I'm not sure, I've never asked him. He might be interested in the computer magnet," mused Maddy.

"You should ask him," suggested Alex.

Maddy changed the subject. "I really was surprised that your name wasn't called this evening. I kept listening for it."

"You should have been listening for your own name," joked Alex.

"That's partly why I missed it," explained Maddy.

"Really?"

"Yes, I was expecting to hear Alexandra -—uh, what is your last name anyway?"

"Feldman," replied Alex, "I couldn't remember your last name either. You know the conversation I heard in the elevator?"

"Yes," answered Maddy.

"That was the name they used, one of them said he liked the 'Schmidt girl's piece', but I didn't think I knew who that was at the time."

"It's just as well, I'd have been too nervous if I knew that."

"But you might not have missed your name," pointed out Alex. Maddy chuckled.

———————◉———————

MICHAEL LAY IN BED unable to fall asleep. He was too wired to sleep. Thoughts kept racing through his mind. His mother would be proud of his top ten status, but she'd be on pins and needles waiting to hear if his piece was going to be published. That would drive him crazy. He wondered how long it would take for the committee to make a final decision. He also wondered what his mother would say after she read his essay, maybe she wouldn't really like folks to read that her son thought of her as a stalker and a liar.

Mostly he kept thinking of Maddy. He took her hand and she didn't jerk it away. That was nice. He could have done better with the kiss though. He shouldn't have announced it: I hate to kiss and run. How corny can you get? And the kiss was too abrupt, he should have taken a little more time. He hoped that Maddy thought he rushed because he wanted to avoid missing curfew. Well, he'd have to do better next time, if there ever was a next time. He was sure Maddy's father would not allow her to go to a movie with him even if his mom drove them.

He imagined the two of them devising clever plans to find ways to be together. Then again maybe her dad wouldn't mind after all. Maybe he was exaggerating the problem. No, he definitely wasn't. He decided again to talk to his mom about the situation. Of course, she would wonder about his sudden interest, but he could just say they got to know each other better at the conference.

She had let him take her by the hand... all the way down the stairwell... they continued to hold hands as they watched the fireworks... her hand was so soft...

Chapter 32

Breakfast of Champions

MADDY AWOKE EARLY. This was her last morning in the hotel and she didn't want to sleep the time away. She dressed and packed quickly then slipped out and headed for the breakfast buffet. She made a point to pass Michael's room but the hallway there was quiet. She wished she had thought to arrange to meet him in the morning at a certain time, but he had left too quickly after his goodnight kiss. She smiled remembering it.

She was surprised when she heard a voice asking if he could join her. It was Mr. Daniels. She invited him to sit and watched him fold his long lanky body into the chair on her left.

"You're up early," he observed.

"You, too," she returned.

"Yes, but I'm old and we old folks have to get up early and work the stiffness out of our aching joints you know."

Maddy smiled. Mr. Daniels was definitely not old.

"I bet your parents will be happy they let you come. You made the top ten, that's pretty good."

"Michael, too," pointed out Maddy.

"Do I know how to recommend good writers or not?" asked Mr. Daniels.

"You sure know how to pick 'em," agreed Maddy.

"You did a great job, Maddy."

"Thanks. When will we know which ones will be published?" asked Maddy.

"The committee is meeting this morning. A final list will be sent to me at the school sometime next week so I guess I'll be the one to let you know."

"Did you get a chance to read any of the other essays?" asked Maddy.

"I read all of them."

"All of them?"

"It was no more than I would read grading an assignment from your class," he reminded her.

"But you're not on the committee, are you?" she asked.

"No, but I was on the proof-reading committee and I wanted to read them. I like to keep up with the attitudes and opinions of all you young whipper-snappers," joked Mr. Daniels.

"Were they as good as Miss Barber said they were?" asked Maddy and immediately worried that it might be an inappropriate question.

"I thought they were," admitted Mr. Daniels, "after all the participants were hand picked by their teachers and principals. It's natural to want your school to be represented by your more talented students."

"I guess, but it seems like some of this stuff could be good for all the students, especially the ones who *don't* like to write. Mr. Rodriguez was so good at helping everybody figure out their topics and it hardly seemed like he was doing any more than just letting us think out loud," praised Maddy.

"I sat in on that session; he did do a good job," agreed Mr. Daniels.

"Later, when I got stuck, he made a simple suggestion that really helped me think about what I wanted to say," she added.

Mr. Daniels nodded.

"And I loved the speaker – uh - the second speaker. The lady who talked to us yesterday was funny; she made a writing career sound like it could be exciting, or at least interesting. I think any of the kids at school could get something out of hearing her talk," insisted Maddy.

"There you go again being insightful, young lady. You're probably right, I'll try to keep that in mind when I have to choose next year's participants," said Mr. Daniels.

Maddy smiled at the compliment. She was relaxed and actually enjoying a conversation with her teacher. Feeling bold she decided to ask him about the chaperone policy.

"Mr. Daniels, I was wondering, what exactly is the policy about parents chaperoning at the conference?"

"Well, the committee strongly suggests that parents be discouraged, but there is no official policy prohibiting them from attending if they insist. I was doing my best to strongly discourage without risking the loss of the student's ability to take part. I knew Michael's mom would never keep him from attending, but I wasn't so sure about your parents."

"So, if one of my parents had wanted to come..." began Maddy.

"Then, I would have extended the same option to Mrs. Evans," finished Mr. Daniels.

"Michael wouldn't have liked that," observed Maddy.

"No, probably not," agreed Mr. Daniels, "and speaking of Michael, I think he's just about finished choosing his selections from the buffet."

"Good morning, early birds," said Michael. He had arrived at the table with his tray overloaded as usual.

Mr. Daniels rose. "Well, I have things to do. I'll leave you two champions to your breakfast."

Michael sat down and began unloading his tray. "Look who's just sitting and talking casually with a teacher; will wonders never cease?"

"What are you talking about?" asked Maddy.

"Nothing at all," said Michael letting the matter drop.

"Mr. Daniels said that we should find out next week which essays are going to be published. He said that he'll probably be the one to let us know," Maddy told him.

"That's good to know, but maybe don't mention it to my mom," said Michael taking a bite out of his breakfast wrap.

Maddy suddenly felt a little shy. She couldn't think of anything else to say. Michael continued eating his breakfast without seeming to notice. After a few moments Maddy stood up with her tray.

"Where are you going?" asked Michael.

"I'm just going to return my tray and maybe get some more juice," replied Maddy.

"Would you get me another OJ?" he asked.

"Sure."

She returned with their drinks and sat down again.

"Don't let me forget to get Alex's phone number so I can text her the pics," he said conversationally.

"I won't."

"Are you okay?" he asked.

"Of course I am. Why wouldn't I be?"

"I don't know, you've gone a bit quiet since Mr. D. left," said Michael.

Maddy sighed.

"It doesn't have to be different just because I kissed you last night," he added.

Sometimes Maddy wished that Michael was not quite so straightforward.

"It feels a little different," she explained.

"I know," he agreed, "but does it feel bad?"

"It feels strange."

"It does?"

"Doesn't it?"

"Maybe I shouldn't have kissed you."

"I wouldn't say that..." objected Maddy.

"No, I know it wasn't the best kiss," said Michael with a theatrical sigh and shake of his head, "I'm sure I can do better."

"Geez," said Maddy.

"What I'll need is practice. Practice, practice, practice," he said with a twinkle.

Maddy groaned and gave him a playful shove. Michael would always be Michael and thank goodness for that.

Chapter 33

Homeward Bound

THE STUDENTS WERE MILLING around the lobby stepping over suitcases and waiting for the bus to arrive. Phone numbers and email addresses were exchanged and promises to keep in touch were made. Miss Barber marched through the group checking off names from the list on her clipboard. Michael was busy using these last few minutes to snap some pictures of some of the coaches and Mr. Daniels. He was pleased with a shot of Miss Barber scolding two boys who were running in the lobby.

Maddy was sorry to leave. She looked around the lobby and wondered if she'd ever have another chance to stay in such a nice place. She had bought a few postcards of the hotel in the gift shop. She wasn't planning to mail them; she just wanted to have them to keep as souvenirs. She had also kept her place card and menu from the banquet, the conference agenda, her name tag, and, of course, her certificate. Michael had promised to make a copy of his photos for her and she was looking forward to making a scrapbook of the conference.

Once again they boarded the bus alphabetically so Michael saved her a seat. Meghan and Allison sat together nearby and Alex took the seat directly across the aisle. The bus was loud with laughter and shouted conversation.

Things got quieter after the bus was underway. Alex fell asleep reading a book. Michael was dozing against the window. Maddy, who had gotten up earlier than any of the others, didn't feel drowsy. She was restless and uneasy and wished she had brought something to read to keep her mind busy.

"Not sleepy?" asked Michael quietly.

"No, but I thought you were going to nap," Maddy whispered back.

"I can sleep later today. I have something for you, actually two somethings, but one is for your sister," he said pulling out a gift bag from the hotel.

Inside the bag was a towel with the hotel logo on it and above it embroidered the words: "I stole this from".

"I bought one for myself, too," he told her smiling.

The second item was a teddy bear wearing a tiny tee shirt that said: "Have a beary nice day".

"Oh, he's so cute!' exclaimed Maddy. Cassie will love it, but you shouldn't have spent money..."

"It's fine," he cut her off in mid protest and raising a finger to his lips as a reminder that most everyone was trying to nap, "my mom always gives me some spending money. It's supposed to be emergency money, but if I still have it at the end of whatever trip I'm on I can spend it on souvenirs or snacks or something. And speaking of snacks I also got us some corn chips and a candy bar for the trip home."

Maddy folded the towel and gave the teddy bear a cuddle. "It was sweet of you to think of Cassie," she said careful to keep her voice low.

"I thought it was fitting that she should get a little something since she was the topic of your essay. Without her, where would you be? You may not have landed in the top ten!"

"I guess so," admitted Maddy.

"You must be really close to your sister, providing all that free babysitting, oops, I mean child care," observed Michael.

Maddy noted that he remembered her warning about calling Cassie a baby.

"She's a good kid," said Maddy.

"And you don't ever want her to find out that sometimes people you trust let you down," paraphrased Michael.

Maddy did not reply. She did not want to talk about her essay.

"Has anyone you trusted ever let you down?" persisted Michael.

It was a simple yes or no question.

"I guess so," admitted Maddy.

"Who was it?' asked Michael.

Maddy couldn't answer. She was suddenly very worried that her essay would be published and lead to more people who wanted to know the answer to that question. She could answer the question, "who?" and Michael would probably assume she was talking about her dad's refusal to let her out of the house except for school. Maddy wasn't even sure she could answer the question of how her trust had become so damaged to her own satisfaction. She didn't have the words. Even if she did, she couldn't see herself speaking them out loud.

"Maddy?" asked Michael.

"I can't talk about this, Michael," she said wearily, "I don't even know how to explain it."

"I'm sorry," said Michael letting her off the hook.

Maddy closed her eyes and rubbed her temples.

"Do you have a headache?" asked Michael.

"A little, maybe I just got up too early."

"Maybe, or maybe it's the bus smell. I had a little headache Thursday and it went away after I got off the bus. Can't you smell it?" asked Michael.

"Yeah, that could be it," said Maddy.

She was a little disappointed. The time was slipping away. She had hoped to talk with Michael all the way home, but not if he kept returning to the topics she wanted to avoid. Suddenly she felt very drowsy. She leaned back into her seat and closed her eyes. Michael pushed the armrest between them into an upright position and invited her to lean on him. She snuggled beneath her sweater and leaned into his shoulder. *This is nice* she thought to herself as she drifted off to a very sound sleep.

When she awoke Michael told her they were nearly home. Several students were beginning to stir and gather their belongings. Maddy sat up and folded her sweater over her lap as she glanced toward the floor trying to locate her backpack. Michael lifted it off the floor for her.

"Thanks," she said, "I hope you weren't too uncomfortable."

He smiled, "I was fine. I have been wondering, though, about a few things."

"Such as?"

"Such as if your dad will let you go to a movie with me, or even without me for that matter," said Michael with his typical candor.

Maddy groaned, "Michael ..."

"I know, I know, I'm starting to remind you of Jessie. And speaking of Jessie, will we tell her about uh, you know?" Michael's straightforward manner faltered.

Maddy had not considered this.

"Let's not tell her right away, she'll probably figure it out on her own soon enough," she decided.

Michael agreed. He looked out the window and saw the mall coming into view.

Chapter 34

Homecoming

"TELL ME EVERYTHING!" insisted Michael's mom as she pulled out of the mall parking lot.

"We had a great time," said Michael, "both Maddy and I were in the top ten, but we don't know yet which essays will be published".

"You were?" she exclaimed, "Why didn't you call to let us know?"

"I wanted to tell you in person," replied Michael with a shrug and a glance toward Maddy.

"When will you find out about the winners?" she asked.

Michael groaned inwardly at her use of the word "winners" as if all the other essays were "losers". "Sometime next week," he answered evasively. He wouldn't tell her that Mr. Daniels would hear first. He imagined her making a nuisance of herself daily until the decision was made known.

"Both Chase students are finalists! That's pretty impressive," she continued, "I'll bet your parents will be proud Maddy."

"Yes ma'am," replied Maddy and then decided to share a little more about the conference since Michael was obviously not interested in reliving the events of the past few days. "They had two speakers, one talked about our essays and the other, on the second day, talked about careers in writing. The lady who talked to us on the second day was very good."

"The first guy was incredibly boring," added Michael.

"We worked in small groups to choose our topics and Michael and I were in Mr. Rodriguez' group – he was very good. I was lucky to get Mr. Rodriguez for my coach, everyone was assigned a mentor to work with us individually," Maddy continued.

"Don't remind me," said Michael.

"Excuse me?" asked Mrs. Evans.

Michael then described his trials with his mentor complete with his version of a little old lady voice. By the time they arrived at Maddy's house he had everyone laughing.

Maddy's homecoming was better attended than her departure. Her father came out and helped her with her suitcase. He and Michael's mother chatted together sharing their enthusiasm over their children's accomplishments.

Cassie wandered out after a few minutes. Maddy introduced her to Michael and gave her the teddy bear.

"Michael bought this for you," she said.

"Really?" asked Cassie.

"Sure," said Michael smiling, "You know, your sister missed you so much she wrote her paper all about you!"

"She did?" asked Cassie brightening.

"Yep, and it was so good she got a special certificate for it. You'll have to ask her to show it to you later," Michael told her.

"Do you like your bear?" asked Maddy.

"Yes," said Cassie in a small voice.

"Remember to say 'thank you' to Michael," she prompted.

"Thank you," said Cassie shyly.

Maddy was a bit surprised by Cassie's reaction. She had expected a bigger welcome and more enthusiasm over her gift.

Michael's mother was calling him to the car. He climbed inside and waved goodbye. Maddy's dad came over and put his arm around her while he waved them out of the driveway. Maddy shrunk ever so slightly under his touch. She felt as though they were posing for Mrs. Evans' benefit. As soon as they were out of sight she ducked out from under his arm and went in the house.

Her mother was sitting on the couch drinking a bottle of beer. College football was playing on the television but she wasn't watching it; she was paging through a sales catalog that had come in the mail. Maddy took in the scene immediately and knew that the household was strained. She called out a hello to her mother as she carried her suitcase through the living room and headed for her bedroom. Cassie followed close behind.

In her room she quickly opened her suitcase and emptied it of its contents. She stowed the dirty clothes in the wicker laundry hamper that sat in the bathroom and then organized the papers and mementos she had saved into a pile. She folded her copy of her essay and stuck it in the pages of one of her school books. She grabbed the pile of mementos from her trip and went to find her mother followed closely by Cassie.

"Hi Mom," she said cheerfully, "I brought some stuff to show you." She sat down and told her all about her weekend showing her the mementos as she described the events she had enjoyed over the past two days. Her father joined them after a few minutes. She did not leave out any of the details concerning the conference. They chuckled over her descriptions of the boring speaker and Michael's writing coach. Her father asked an occasional question and seemed genuinely interested in everything she had to say. Her mother perked up when she told them about how her roommates had helped her pull together an outfit for the banquet and was happy to hear that Michael was going to give her copies of his photos. By the time she had described missing the calling of her name at the banquet things seemed more like normal.

"So when are you going to show us your paper?" asked her father.

"I forgot to get a copy," she lied.

"How could you forget?" he sputtered.

"Oh, because it was done on a computer and the printer was shared by several stations," she answered smoothly, "I just ran out of time. Anyway, I know we'll get a free copy of the magazine when it comes out."

"Dear, she probably just forgot in all the excitement," soothed her mother.

"We'll have to get several copies of the magazine when it comes out," said her father, "I can't wait to show Mr. Pearson at the store."

"Well, I still have school work to catch up on," concluded Maddy, "I'm gonna work on it for a while, okay?"

"Sure, honey," said her mother.

"Want to come with me, Cassie?" she asked her sister.

"Yeah," answered Cassie.

Maddy sat with Cassie on her bed. She showed her the postcards that she had bought and described her hotel room and the swimming pool. Cassie was wide-eyed at the idea of a swimming pool with slides. Maddy had even kept the original hotel brochure with its glossy pictures of the pool. She watched while Cassie pored over the pictures.

"So, did you miss me?" she asked.

"Yeah," Cassie replied simply.

"What did you do while I was gone," Maddy asked.

Cassie shrugged, "Not much."

Maddy was worried. Her mother was clearly upset about something. She hadn't even come outside to welcome her home. At first she had supposed she was out doing errands and was concerned to see her on the couch when she came in. She seemed some better after their conversation although the beer was disturbing. Both her parents enjoyed an occasional drink but usually her mother drank with a meal and she had never seen her drink straight from a bottle.

Cassie's behavior was even more disturbing. Maddy had expected her to give Michael a giant hug after receiving the teddy bear and was puzzled when she did not. She had expected Cassie to have lots of questions, but she hadn't interrupted once during Maddy's conversation with her parents. She turned to look at her sister who was now occupying herself with her Barbie dolls.

"Cassie, when I finish my school work we'll take a walk, okay?" she told her.

"Okay," said Cassie.

Maddy sighed. That wasn't the reply she had hoped for either. Where was the enthusiasm she had written about in her paper? Where was the curiosity? All that seemed to remain of the qualities outlined in her essay was patience, a quiet, resigned sort of patience.

Chapter 35

Manipulating Michael

———◦———

"MADDY'S FATHER SEEMS like a nice fellow," said Michael's mother as she backed out of the Schmidt's driveway.

"Humph," snorted Michael.

"What is that supposed to mean, young man?" asked Mrs. Evans.

Michael knew his mother would not appreciate rudeness directed toward an adult even if he had waited to express it until they were on their way. He was being raised to be a polite young man, one who does not grunt first of all and, secondly, one who does not criticize his elders. Michael wanted to say, "He's a jerk, Mom!" but resisted the impulse since name-calling would not make any points with his mother.

"Mom, did you know he almost didn't let Maddy go to the conference?" he asked.

His mother did not reply at first. She seemed to be choosing her words carefully.

"Well, I heard that he had some concerns," she admitted.

"He never lets her do anything. Not parties or activities or anything," he complained.

"How can you be sure of that?" she asked.

"We're friends, Mom, she told me. She said she was afraid up until the very last second that he would change his mind. You can ask Mr. Daniels: she even considered writing her essay about the fact that her dad almost didn't let her go," he revealed.

"That probably wouldn't have been a very good idea," she observed.

Michael's stomach did a momentary flip at her comment. He prayed she wouldn't feel the same way about being the subject of his own paper. Still, he stayed focused on his topic.

"Mom, he wouldn't let her join the scouts or the soccer team..." he began.

"Michael," she interrupted, "honey, maybe they can't afford it."

Michael was unconvinced. He knew he could build a case if she would just listen. "She is never allowed to go to birthday parties, or *any* kind of party. I'm not the only one who's noticed either. Jessie has invited her for sleepovers lots of times but she's never allowed to go," he continued.

"People are more careful these days about who they leave their children with," she offered, "You know how I insist on meeting your friends' parents before you can visit them in their homes."

Michael privately considered that she had just met Mr. Schmidt and misjudged him badly. True, he had been pleasant enough in a small talk aren't-our-kids-wonderful kind of way, but anyone can be charming for a few minutes. An idea began to suggest itself and he decided to try it out.

"I bet if I invited Maddy to do something next Saturday, he would say no," he challenged.

"What would you invite her to do?" she asked.

"Oh, I don't know," said Michael as if he hadn't any specific idea, "maybe to a movie or something."

"I'll do you one better," said his mother thoughtfully, "I'll do the inviting. It may make them more comfortable if the invitation is offered by an adult. It will give them a chance to get to know me a little bit and ease their minds."

"Okay," said Michael, "but don't be surprised when they say no."

"Let's just wait and see what happens," she said.

Michael smiled to himself at how easily that was accomplished. *Well played, Michael, well played.*

Chapter 36

"Phonophobia"

MRS. EVANS KEPT HER promise. She called a few days later to invite Maddy to a movie to celebrate her accomplishment. Mrs. Schmidt thanked her for the invitation and said she would talk it over with her husband. The following day Mr. Schmidt called to regretfully decline due to a previous commitment.

Mrs. Evans was undeterred. Not long after she called again to invite Maddy to accompany the Evans family on an outing to a museum featuring exhibits on famous American writers. She was keeping with the "budding writer's theme" offering it as an acknowledgement of Maddy and Michael's success at the conference. Again Mrs. Schmidt thanked her and deferred to her husband who later phoned with regrets.

Her final attempt was an invitation to a ballet of Romeo and Juliet being produced by a local ballet company. Mr. Daniel's class was reading the play and she suggested that it might help them better understand the story since Shakespeare's 17th century language might be difficult for the seventh graders. She even gave them a choice of *three* dates since she unfortunately seemed to be unlucky with her timing. When even this offer was refused she decided to give up wondering if she might be making things difficult for Maddy with her persistence.

It was, indeed, making life very stressful in the Schmidt household. By the third invitation the sound of the telephone seemed to rattle the entire household. Maddy's mother began to complain that she wished Mrs. Evans would call in the evenings when her husband was at home. She had already explained twice that she had to talk these things over with her husband. Couldn't the woman get the message?

Maddy knew that her mother was being put in a position that was uncomfortable for her. For one thing she hated talking on the phone. It was a family joke that she had "phonophobia". If Maddy was home she answered the phone shooing off salesmen or charity solicitations. In the evenings Maddy's father always took any calls that came in. An additional reason for her discomfort was the fact that she had to continue to raise the subject of the invitations with her husband.

Maddy's father was getting more upset with each call from Mrs. Evans.

"Next time you see her name on caller ID just ignore the damn woman!" he instructed.

Usually Maddy's invitations came through her friends at school. She would ask her dad, wait for the inevitable reply, and finally respond in person to her friend. Her parents need never be involved in the process. A personal invitation from a parent was a new wrinkle, one her parents were finding troublesome.

Not all phone calls to the house were unwelcome, however. On the Friday after the conference Mr. Daniels called and asked to speak to her mother. He told her that Maddy's essay had been chosen for publication in the local paper. Maddy listened as her mother's voice changed from her unnatural sounding "Hello" to an excited, "That's wonderful!"

The most surprising news of the phone call was that the panel had decided to publish *four* articles instead of three. One of the students had turned her paper in after the deadline and was at first not eligible for consideration. After reading her essay the committee members learned that it had been turned in only minutes late and then after technical problems she had tried to resolve on her own. It was well written and most certainly would have been chosen had it been received on time. Not wanting to "bump" one of the original three finalists the committee decided the best and easiest solution was to publish an additional essay.

Maddy was sure that it had to be Alex's essay, but her mother couldn't remember the names of the other writers.

"Was Michael Evans chosen?" asked Maddy.

"Yes, he was mentioned and another boy named Jason something and you and... another boy I can't remember," said her mother.

"Was it Alex Feldman maybe?"

"That's it."

"That's Alexandra, Mom! She was my roommate! This is so cool! I wonder if Michael knows yet. Can I call him?" babbled Maddy.

"Not right now, Mr. Daniels might be trying to reach his folks," her mother sounded defensive.

Maddy was absolutely certain that Mr. Daniels had called the Evans' house first. She understood that her mother was objecting to initiating any contact with the Evans family. And this was after only one invitation had been extended. Maddy's disappointment was short lived; Michael called her only a few moments later to share his excitement.

"Did you hear?" he asked.

"Yes! Isn't it great about Alex?"

"Yeah, I wish I'd read hers now."

"You will soon enough."

"Do you know when it will be in the paper?"

"Mr. D. told my mom it's gonna be the first Sunday in January. One each Sunday for four weeks like a special series. We're gonna be interviewed, too!"

"We are? I didn't hear about that."

"Someone is supposed to phone to set up a time."

A phone call, terrific, my mother will be delighted to hear it.

Chapter 37

Special Assignment

MR. DANIELS CHOSE THE Monday after Thanksgiving break to ruin his students' holiday spirits. Michael and Jessie groaned all the way to the cafeteria. Maddy was amused by the amount of effort they put into their protests; it was just an assignment after all.

"Poetry!" exclaimed Michael with disgust.

"It's bad enough we have to read it and try to understand that junk," complained Jessie, "now he wants us to write a poem."

"Geez!" spat Michael as he pulled a sandwich from his lunch bag.

"I can't write a poem," said an already defeated Jessie.

"Come on, guys," said Maddy, "it won't be that bad."

"I hate Mr. Daniels!" insisted Jessie ripping grapes from their stems.

"No, you don't," said Maddy reasonably.

"Well, he's definitely turned to the dark side with this assignment," said Michael.

"And it's due Friday! That's no time at all!" worried Jessie.

Maddy decided it was time for a change of subject.

"Jessie, are you going to be able to come with us for the interview on Saturday?" she asked.

Jessie had proposed a feature for the school news show covering the interviews of Chase Middle School's outstanding writers. Mr.

Buchanan nixed the idea saying he didn't want to impose on the *Times*. The reporter was expecting to be the interviewer not the interviewee. Jessie had countered that she didn't need to record the interview or even question the reporter, she just wanted to listen in and take some notes. She planned to shoot footage of Maddy and Michael entering the newspaper offices. In spite of her best efforts Mr. Buchanan limited her coverage to an on-campus interview with the students only.

"Nah, Mr. Buchanan wouldn't go for it," she replied, "It's too bad, too; it was going to be my reward for writing this stupid poem."

Maddy sighed.

"Besides," Jessie continued, "the big question is: "Will your parents allow *you* to go, Maddy?"

"Yes," said Maddy making an effort not to be offended by the question, "my dad is going to drop me off on his way to work and I told him I could take the bus home."

"We could drive you home," offered Michael.

"Listen, I gotta go early today and pay a library fine," interrupted Jessie, "my mom made me promise not to put it off any longer." She quickly gathered her backpack and scooped up her trash.

"Want me to come with you?" offered Maddy.

"Well, duh, you're still eating," Jessie replied noting the obvious. She climbed over the bench and waved the hand that was clutching her trash at them as if to say, "don't be silly."

After she left Michael repeated his offer, "We'd be happy to drive you home, Maddy".

"I know, but I'm not sure what my parents would say," she replied frankly.

Michael was quiet. He was disappointed and discouraged. The closeness they had enjoyed at the conference was beginning to feel like a dream. They hadn't needed to worry about hiding anything from Jessie; everything was just as it had been before the conference. They were back to being classmates and friends, which wasn't bad but it wasn't what he wanted. More than that, Maddy's isolation, which had always been an unacknowledged fact of life, was becoming impossible for him to ignore. He knew his mother had concerns as well although she didn't share them with him.

"What your parents don't know won't hurt you," he said defiantly.

"What?"

"They don't have any idea how long the interviews will take. We can drop you off near your house. They don't even have to know we gave you a lift. You can save the bus fare," he schemed.

"Your mom would wonder why she couldn't drop me off at my house," she objected.

"No, she wouldn't, not anymore, your dad has already refused enough invitations from her, she's beginning to get the idea," he said flatly.

Maddy looked stricken. She stood and began to gather her books and clean up after herself.

"I'm sorry," said Michael meaning it. He had gone too far. He took her hand hoping she would sit back down, but it was too late. She yanked it back and stormed out far more comfortable pretending anger than showing the sadness and anxiety that had been growing over the past few weeks.

Chapter 38

Cassie Speaks

MADDY HAD FINISHED her homework, except for the poem she had to write. The beginning had seemed to come from nowhere:

In our house,
We all are friends.
All is well,
No one offends.

She stared at the words wondering what to write next. Michael and Jessie's attitude about the assignment made more sense to her now. She was vaguely aware that what she had written was a lie. After a few minutes she threw it away and tried to write a poem about something else, anything else. She wrote a few lines about a flower – it was forced and sing-songy and she threw it away, too. Her original thought was persistent. She wrote it down again and sure enough more words came:

We do our jobs
To school we go,
To work, to church,
To learn to grow.

She rearranged the second line to read: "We go to school". She reread the first three lines and crossed out the last line. She thought for a moment before adding, "They all are fooled", in its place. That would never do! She tore the sheet of paper out of its wire binding and wadded it into a ball. She noted the familiar beginnings of a headache and pushed her work aside. She wasn't worried; it wasn't due until Friday.

She went into the kitchen to take something for her head. Her mother was there just finishing washing Cassie's hair over the kitchen sink. Cassie was kneeling on a kitchen chair. Maddy shook two pills out of a bottle and got a glass; she waited as her mother finished the final rinse and wrapped Cassie's long hair into a towel with a sigh.

Maddy filled her glass with water as soon as she could get to the faucet. She quickly popped the pills with a swallow of water.

"I would have done that, Mom," she said.

"Oh, it's okay," replied her mother, "I don't mind." Maddy knew that wasn't true but she didn't argue the point. She turned her attention to Cassie instead, "Come on, Cassie, I'll comb out your hair for you."

In their room Maddy began the tedious process of combing out her sister's long brown hair. She carefully held the hair so that the comb would not pull at the roots. Cassie was less quiet than when Maddy first returned from the conference, but still not quite her usual perky self. Maddy talked to her about school but her replies showed little of Cassie's usual color and detail. Maddy asked her if anything was wrong and she said no and went quiet. Uncomfortable with the change in her sister, she talked to Cassie about her poetry assignment. Cassie asked to see it.

Encouraged that Cassie seemed interested Maddy found the wadded-up pages in the trash. She read the poem about the flower to Cassie first.

"What do you think?" she asked her sister.

Cassie shrugged, "It's okay."

"Cassie, is something wrong?" she asked for a second time.

"No," came the simple reply. Cassie did not meet her eyes.

Maddy sighed. She reached into the wastebasket and withdrew the crumpled ball that was her earliest attempt at her assignment. She opened the page and smoothed the wrinkles. Her uneasiness slowly transformed itself into a concrete thought. She read those four lines to Cassie: In our house, we all are friends, all is well, no one offends.

Cassie's eyes narrowed. "What does 'no one offends' mean?" she asked.

"It means no one hurts anyone else," she answered.

"You mean like pinches?"

Maddy smiled and explained, "Well, it could be pinches, they can hurt. It could also mean hurting someone's feelings. I guess there are lots of ways to offend someone."

Cassie was quiet again. Maddy needed to confirm her suspicions but she didn't know how to ask. "Cassie, remember when I went away to the conference?" she asked.

"Yes."

"What did you do while I was gone?"

"Went to school."

"What did you do at home?"

"I don't know."

"Did you do anything special?"

"Daddy said it was special."

Maddy's heart sank. She was reeling. She never should have left her. Never. It was her fault; it was all her fault. She had been selfish to go, only thinking of herself and what she wanted.

"He played the special game that he plays with you at night time. He said I was big enough to play now," continued Cassie, "I said I didn't want to play; I was too tired to play." Maddy didn't want to hear anymore, but she needed to know a little more.

"Was that the first time you ever played that game with Daddy?" she asked as though they were talking about the weather.

"Yes," came the reply.

Maddy sighed before asking her last question: "How many times have you played this game with Daddy?"

"Two times." *Two nights, two times.*

"Have you played since I came home?"

"No." *No, thank God, no. Good, that's good.*

Maddy braided Cassie's hair. When she finished, she told Cassie that she was a good girl to be so patient while she combed her hair. She also told her not to worry about playing the game anymore, she would work something out. Cassie did not reply, but seemed more cheerful after that. They did not talk again about the subject.

Chapter 39

Kiss and Make Up

BY THURSDAY MADDY COULD put it off no longer: she had to write her poem. She sat on her bed in her room determined to finish it. "In our house, we all are friends" she wrote. She crossed out "we all are friends" and wrote "we all pretend" in its place. "That all is well, no one offends." That was better. At least it was truthful. She had no intention of turning in the poem that she wrote, but it seemed as though she needed to write it. She marveled at how easily the words came once she let them. After she was finished, she reworked it into another much shorter poem that she planned to turn in to Mr. Daniels.

The poems were turned in on Friday. Jessie continued to worry over her grade even after it was turned in, but Michael's mood improved immediately. It was not in his nature to brood after the fact. Maddy was not happy with her poem, but did not really care.

Michael had noticed a dramatic change in her that week. She looked tired and was more withdrawn than usual, skipping lunch a couple of times to work in the library instead of joining them in the cafeteria. He felt sure she was avoiding him and regretted Monday's lunchtime conversation. He told Jessie what had happened.

"Good!" she said, "maybe with both of us putting on pressure, she'll finally do something about her situation!"

"Jessie, it's not that easy; it's not like standing up to a school bully, this is her dad we're talking about," he said. Then he explained how hard his mother had tried to invite her on an outing. "Every time she spoke to Maddy's mom and every time her mom said she had to ask Maddy's dad. Even her mother seems afraid to give permission on her own. Her dad would call back later to say she couldn't go."

"Wow," admitted Jessie, "that is bad."

"It's a miracle she even went to the conference," he told her.

"I really came down hard on her about the soccer team," Jessie regretted aloud.

"It was important to you," said Michael, understanding his friend.

"Man," said Jessie, "They turned your mom down three times? That's amazing! No one ever says 'no' to your mother."

"Here she comes," warned Michael.

Maddy joined them at the table.

"What's up?" she asked.

"We're just rejoicing that the poem is turned in," said Jessie.

"Thank God!" said Maddy with feeling, "I'm glad that's over with."

"But you said it was just another assignment, oh exalted-almost-published-writer!" protested Jessie.

"Well, I was wrong about that," admitted Maddy.

The three of them enjoyed a good long gripe session about Mr. Daniels and his unfair assignment. They made all the usual arguments that students make about particularly challenging assignments: "We'll never use this in real life," and "He better not grade too hard; who's to say what's good poetry and what's not?" Their arguments were punctuated with such thoughtful remarks as,

"Poetry sucks" and "Mr. Daniels probably couldn't write a poem if his life depended on it." Eventually they ran out of steam and turned to other topics.

"Tomorrow should be interesting," said Michael.

"Yeah, I wish I could be there," said Jessie unhappily, "at least Mr. Daniels said we could use class time on Monday for my interview with you for Chase News," said Jessie.

"That's good," said Maddy, "Michael, do you think you could give me a ride home tomorrow after all?"

"Sure," said Michael brightening, "uh, listen, I'm sorry about the other day…"

"It's okay," Maddy cut him off, "I'm sorry I stormed out like I did. I was overreacting."

"Well, I was being pushy," admitted Michael.

"Okay enough of that stuff," interrupted Jessica. Now that you've kissed and made up, maybe things can get back to normal around here."

Chapter 40

Maddy Decides

MADDY LAY IN BED WAITING and thinking. She was tired and wanted to sleep, but she couldn't yet. She had remained awake every night since her talk with Cassie, dreading the sound of her father's footsteps down the hall and hoping instead to hear him snoring in his bedroom nearby. She was grateful for his loud snore which could be heard in every corner of the small house.

She considered what she would do if he came. Probably it would be okay; he would come to her as always. But she worried about what she could do if he instead went to her sister's bed. She decided she would have to let him know she was awake, if he knew maybe he wouldn't bother her. But what if Cassie was what he wanted, what if he insisted on Cassie? She tried to imagine confronting him, standing up to him, protecting her sister, but couldn't think of a single thing she could say to him to stop him. Her usual ways of coping would not work in this situation, she could not withdraw.

Maddy cringed as she remembered Cassie's voice, "*He played the special game that he plays with you*". In spite of her efforts to protect Cassie, she had known. She was upset to think that her baby sister had been awake some nights when he had come. That she had listened and maybe even watched him with her. Smart

Cassie; somehow she had known to remain quiet, that it was a secret thing.

Maddy had decided that she would have to tell if she were going to protect Cassie. She remembered the promise included in her essay and meant to keep it, to make up for what she had done to her sister. Who could she tell? Who could help? Who would believe her? What words would she use to express her problem?

The interviews were scheduled for the morning. She would get to see Alex again since all four finalists were being interviewed. Should she tell Alex just to see her reaction? No, she did not know her well enough. Jessie would not be there. She knew she would choose Michael; that was why she had asked him for a ride home. Michael would, of course, tell his mother. Would she believe him? Would she even know what to do? Maybe she wouldn't do anything at all. Michael had said that his mother was beginning to get the picture, Maddy was doubtful about that. How could she possibly know that the picture was this ugly?

Chapter 41

Reunion

MADDY'S FATHER DROPPED her off in front of the downtown offices of the newspaper. He had been in a jolly mood that morning even stopping at McDonald's drive-through to buy her an Egg McMuffin and juice.

He was always interested in her school work and her grades were usually good which Maddy decided made him feel good about himself. He had told Maddy many times about how he never finished high school, dropping out when his father died to get a job to help support his mother and sisters. An education was important to him and he was determined to make sure his daughters went to college.

They talked that morning about the math test she had aced the day before and the poem she had struggled all week to write. When he dropped her off, he told her where she could pick up the bus that would take her home. He warned her not to talk to anyone on the bus.

Maddy climbed out of the car and watched him drive off. He had been so happy in the car, she almost felt normal with him. She wished things could be different; she wished *he* could be different. At least she could enjoy the morning knowing he was at work, not at home with Cassie.

She turned her attention to the task at hand and looked up and down the street wondering if the others were inside or if she was the first to arrive. Her watch said she was early so she decided to wait a few minutes before going inside. Somewhat nervous, Maddy looked around hoping to spot Michael or Alex. She had been counting on Michael being there so they could find their way together. At last, she saw him coming from down the block with his mom and waved to them.

Maddy was glad for once when Mrs. Evans joined them and led the way to the information counter for assistance. After a brief chat with the receptionist, she accompanied them to the elevators. They met up with Alex and Jason, the fourth finalist, in a waiting area on the fifth floor. The parents were asked to remain in the waiting area while the students were escorted to a different room and told that the reporter would arrive shortly. An assistant explained that they would be interviewed individually and could leave when they were finished.

They interviewed Jason first at his request; he had football practice that morning and hoped to get away as soon as possible.

"Here we are together again!" said Michael cheerfully.

Alex was eyeing Maddy critically. "You look terrible," she told her, "Is everything alright?"

Maddy was surprised by Alex's assessment. She hadn't considered that the stress and lack of rest of the previous week might affect her appearance. She looked up to see Michael studying his feet while Alex waited for her reply.

"I guess I haven't been sleeping well lately," she said lamely.

"It's been just awful," Michael stepped in, "we've been suffering mightily under the oppression of Mr. Daniels' evil poetry assignment this week."

Maddy breathed a sigh of relief and added, "We had to write a poem and it was harder to do than I thought. I was up late a couple of nights trying to finish it."

"She's such a perfectionist," put in Michael.

Alex looked doubtful but let it pass. She told them how surprised she had been to hear from the committee.

"I knew your paper was good," insisted Maddy, "I told you I was waiting to hear them call your name."

"Yes, you did," agreed Alex, "I thought you were trying to make me feel better."

"I wasn't cheering you up because you didn't seem upset," said Maddy.

"Oh, I wasn't devastated, just disappointed. After all, I didn't even think I was in the top ten and I had worked so hard," Alex explained.

"I know, I couldn't believe it when you didn't make it," repeated Maddy.

"Well, it doesn't seem like such a big deal now, there are bigger problems to face," said Alex.

"Such as?" asked Michael.

"Nana died the Friday before Thanksgiving," Alex told them sadly.

"Oh, I'm so sorry," said Maddy.

"That's too bad," added Michael.

"They said she died in her sleep and that it was peaceful. I keep wondering why they think they know that if no one was with her," said Alex.

The door opened and the assistant called Alex away.

"Well, that was bad timing," noted Michael who had offered to go first but was told that the reporter hoped to talk briefly with both Chase students together. Alex waved away the offer and said she would be fine.

"Do I really look terrible?" Maddy asked Michael.

"You look a little tired," said Michael frankly, "I've been kinda worried about you."

"I'm okay, but it's been a horrible week. You and Jessica are right; I really do need to do something about my situation at home. I just don't know what." Maddy knew she wasn't going to be able to talk to Michael about this.

"Maybe my mom would be helpful," suggested Michael, "she's already worried about you."

"She is? Why?" asked Maddy, surprised.

"It's just lots of little things. The fact that your parents didn't want you to go to the conference doesn't make any sense to her at all. Then, when your parents didn't see you off the morning of the bus trip, she just didn't know what to make of that. And of course there were all the invitations. Your mom didn't seem to be able to make a decision without checking with your dad first. All together it just makes her concerned," Michael explained.

Maddy was in no mood to argue. The idea that Michael's mother was worried about her was oddly appealing.

"Not being allowed to do things is just part of the problem though," she said.

Michael was beginning to understand that Maddy's problem was going to prove to be too big for him to solve. In a few minutes Alex came out and told Maddy they wanted to see her next.

"Now, what's wrong with you?" demanded Alex after Maddy left. "You look like someone just slapped you."

"Alex, when did you get to be so blunt?" asked Michael.

"I've always been blunt, you just don't know me very well," she replied.

"That's true," he admitted, "I don't really know anything except that Maddy is upset about her dad. She didn't say much more than that."

"I knew it wasn't just some silly poetry assignment. She looks terrible."

"So you said."

"Maybe I'll give her a call this week," said Alex, "I'll just tell her I want to talk about Nana and maybe she'll tell me more about what's up with her. I can't stay; my mom is turning this into a kind of mother-daughter day. By the way, are you two still ...?" Alex didn't feel the need to finish her thought.

"Not exactly," he replied.

"Sorry to hear it," she said, meaning it.

Michael followed Alex to the room where the parents were waiting. He gestured to his mother and she stepped into the hall.

"Are you finished?" she asked.

"No. Mom, Maddy is upset about something and asked if we could talk somewhere after the interview. She didn't say exactly, but it's something about her dad. Can you take us to the mall for lunch and give me a little time with her to see if she'll tell me what's wrong?" he was whispering.

Michael's mother rubbed her temples and closed her eyes thinking for a moment before answering, "I'm not comfortable with this Michael."

"It's not much different from driving her to the same mall where we caught the bus for the conference, is it?" he challenged.

"You know it is, Kiddo."

"Mom, something's wrong. Maddy's parents think she's taking the bus, but they don't know exactly when to expect her."

"Why can't her dad pick her up?"

"He's working."

"I'll call her mom."

"But, Mom..."

"It's the best I can do, Michael."

Chapter 42

Michael Makes a Suggestion

MADDY COULD TELL BY the reporter's face that he found her essay far more interesting than its author. They talked a little about school and the topic of her essay, Cassie. Her replies were short and flat sounding. She responded to his questions about the conference more fully. She even repeated her comments to Mr. Daniels about how she thought the conference might be especially helpful to students who don't like to write.

Things picked up when Michael came into the room. The reporter wanted to know if all Chase Middle School students were talented writers since both of them had been chosen for publication. Michael responded to most of the questions and soon had the reporter chuckling. After a few minutes Maddy was allowed to step out.

Back in the room where she had waited, Maddy wondered if she should go find Michael's mother or stay there and wait for Michael. She considered leaving altogether to find the bus stop. What would she say to Michael? She should have told Alex; it would be easier to talk about this to a girl She needed to do something and she would do something, but was this the right thing?

She stopped pacing when Michael stepped back into the room.

"Everything was alright," Mrs Evans told them at the car. She had phoned Maddy's house and told her mother that she was taking them for a quick lunch when they finished and promised to drive Maddy home immediately afterward.

At the mall they went to the food court and after they were all settled with their trays Michael's mother excused herself to do some shopping.

"We only have about half an hour," Michael prompted.

Maddy considered that it was not nearly enough time. She thought she might cry and was afraid that once she started she might never stop. She wasn't hungry but took a bite of her sandwich to delay the conversation for a few moments more.

"You can tell me, Maddy," he said gently, "remember when I told you about my brother on the bus? I'd never told anyone else about him."

"This isn't like that," she said softly.

"Okay." Michael waited.

"I should never have gone to the conference," she said finally.

"Of course you should have," Michael insisted, "and you have the certificate to prove it."

"That's not what I mean."

"What do you mean?" Michael couldn't understand why she didn't just come out with it. They had disagreed about similar things in the past. Maddy often accused him of being too straightforward while he found her hesitancy to speak up frustrating.

"I shouldn't have left Cassie alone," she said sadly.

"She wasn't alone," he objected, confused, "she was with your mom and dad for cripes sake. You're her sister, not her *mother*, Maddy."

"I know," admitted Maddy, "but my mom doesn't..."

"Did something happen to Cassie? She looked fine to me," said Michael.

Maddy stared at her plate. "Michael, I just can't explain this to you, I - I don't know how to say it."

Michael had a thought. "Maybe you don't have to say it; maybe you can write it instead. Maybe when you get it down on paper it'll be easier. Remember my notebook? It really did help even though I never meant for my mom to see it."

Maddy brightened. She liked the idea. She could write it for practice and then maybe even read it if she had to. People are less likely to interrupt if you read something to them. She could say everything all at once and it would be over.

"I could write it," she mused aloud, "but who could I read it to?"

"Read it to me and then we'll decide together what to do," offered Michael taking her hand.

Maddy smiled. That was very like Michael: practical and dependable.

"Do it soon, Maddy," said Michael.

Maddy thought a moment. She didn't say so, but in a way, maybe she had already written it.

Chapter 43

Mrs. Evans has Questions

"SO?" ASKED MICHAEL'S mother after they dropped off Maddy, "did you find anything out?"

"No," said Michael, "but maybe I'll know more soon."

"Can you tell me what she did say?" she asked.

"She said she shouldn't have gone to the conference, that she shouldn't have left her sister. It doesn't make any sense."

Mrs. Evans was quiet. Michael knew she was making an effort to keep her thoughts to herself. He knew she would resist making any sort of judgment without being sure of her facts. Just this once he wished she would let him in on her thoughts.

Michael had no idea about whatever it was that was troubling Maddy. Nothing she had said made any sense to him. Her father was a jerk and her mother was a wimp and she was caught in the middle. She seemed to think she was responsible for her sister even when she wasn't at home.

Michael's mother interrupted his thoughts.

"Didn't you get to read her essay, Michael?"

"Yeah, and Mr. Daniels read it, too. Man, I wish I had a copy of it to show you. I can't remember it exactly, but in the last couple of paragraphs she worries that her sister might lose the qualities she admires and promises to try to protect her or something. She

183

wrote that sometimes people you trust let you down and I asked her about that after I finished reading it."

"What did she say?"

"She wouldn't talk about it. And I asked her more than once."

"Maybe I should have talked with her for a few minutes."

"I don't think it would've worked. She keeps saying she doesn't know how to explain it," Michael said.

"I wonder if I should bring this up with the school counselor," she mused.

"Not yet, Mom," said Michael, alarmed at the idea. "She's supposed to tell me something soon."

"How soon?" she asked.

"Monday, I hope. Please, Mom, don't say anything yet," he pleaded.

"Alright," she said, "I really don't know anything for sure anyway."

Michael nudged the conversation in a slightly different direction.

"How did you get Maddy's mom to agree to lunch?"

"Oh, that wasn't too hard," she told him.

"Really? She hasn't been able to make any decisions about your other invitations," said Michael surprised.

"I didn't ask her to decide, I just *told* her what I was going to do and waited to see if she would object. I had a hunch she wouldn't."

Well played, Mom, well played.

Chapter 44

A Midnight Snack

MADDY'S FATHER OPENED the door very quietly and tiptoed inside. Maddy noted with alarm that he was heading for Cassie's side of the room. She sat up, her heart pounding.

"Is something wrong?" she asked.

"I was just checking on Cassie," he whispered.

"She's fine," hissed Maddy, "Don't wake her or she'll never settle down. Then she'll keep me up all night." She was trying hard to make it sound as if this might be an ongoing problem with her annoying sister. She was also worried that Cassie was playing possum and might give herself away.

Her mind was spinning. Should she challenge him or play along? It was his move.

"Well, I guess she's fine," he said finally, "How are you doing?"

He turned toward her side of the room. She *willed* him to her side. A small part of her was aware of how odd it felt to want him to come to her, if only to keep him away from Cassie. Her heart skipped a beat when Cassie stirred. Her father appeared not to notice. He sat down on the edge of her bed.

"Turn on your back," he told her. Maddy did as she was told.

Cassie sat up and rubbed her eyes. "What's wrong, Daddy?" she asked.

Maddy's heart sank. She wondered what he would do.

"Nothing is wrong sweetie," soothed her father.

"I want a drink of water," insisted Cassie. Maddy was screaming inside. This was not supposed to happen. How could she protect her if she couldn't stay quiet?

"Okay, baby, let's go get a drink in the kitchen."

They left together. Maddy could think of nothing else but to follow them pretending a similar thirst.

Maddy considered the midnight snack a minor miracle. In the kitchen their father decided to put on some milk to warm and cut three pieces of pound cake from the loaf on top of the refrigerator. They sat together and talked about cartoons while they snacked. Cassie chose the topic. When the last crumbs were cleaned up they were put back to bed.

"We can't stay up all night," said their dad, "we've got church tomorrow."

A few moments after he left Maddy felt Cassie crawl into bed with her. She tucked her in and told her to go to sleep. Even after she heard the now comforting sound of her father's snore she couldn't sleep.

She had decided who and when she would tell and went over her plan in her mind. She was going to take a page out of Michael's book and open the topic with what she had written. She tried to imagine how she might answer the questions that were sure to follow. She did not allow herself to imagine anything else.

Chapter 45

Maddy "Speaks"

MADDY WAS EARLY TO school on Monday. It was part of her plan. She was surprised to see Michael nervously pacing in the hall outside of Mr. Daniels' room. His mother was inside.

"Hi, Maddy," said Michael.

"Uh oh," said Maddy, "this isn't Wednesday. Is your mom up to her old habits?"

"Maybe," said Michael.

"Think we'll get our poems back today?" she asked changing the subject.

"I hope not," said Michael with a grimace.

Maddy was distracted by the idea that her plan was already off course. She suddenly realized that she hadn't allowed enough time, after school would be better. She was afraid that she might not go through with it if she had to wait until the end of the day. She wanted to get it over with.

"Did you write anything over the weekend?" asked Michael.

"No," said Maddy truthfully.

"When are you going to do it? Or did you change your mind?" he asked.

"I don't know, soon," she assured him.

Michael's mother stepped into the hall.

"Oh, hello, dear," she said, "It's good to see you again."

"Good morning," said Maddy.

"Are you here to see me?" asked Mr. Daniels.

"Uh, yes, but I think the bell's gonna ring," she told him.

Mrs. Evans excused herself and told Michael to get to class. Mr. Daniels asked Maddy to step inside for a moment and closed the door.

"Maddy, what do you have second period?" he asked.

"Algebra with Mr. Cuervo," she replied.

"Ask him for a pass and come see me if you can; I want to talk to you about your poem," he said.

"Can't you just talk to me in class?" she asked.

"I could, but I'd rather spend a little more time on the conversation than class time allows. Don't worry so much, I promise it will all be constructive criticism," he smiled.

"Yes, sir," she replied.

"Don't forget," he made her promise.

She stepped out into a very crowded hall. Mr. Daniels' first period class was milling about waiting to enter his room. She made her way through them as they pushed forward through the doorway.

First period seemed to go on forever. Mr. Ernst droned on and on writing notes on the smart board for the students to copy down. Maddy kept up with the notes but paid little attention to his lecture. She wasn't worried; the test would come from the notes and chapter vocabulary as always. When the bell finally rang, she jumped with a start and began to gather her things before realizing that it was only the first bell. Class would not be dismissed until after the morning show. She slumped back into her seat and put her head down on her desk to wait.

She was almost disappointed when Mr. Cuervo gave her a hall pass without question and told her to take all the time she needed. She stopped at her locker on her way and dropped off her math and science texts. She took a sheet out of her language arts book and put it in her language arts folder. She was ready.

Mr. Daniels asked her to step in and pull up a chair. He did not close the door since he was not expecting a class. Maddy sat and waited while he searched for her poem on his desk.

"It's here someplace," he said chuckling, "It's just a matter of finding it in this mess." She knew he was trying to put her at ease and was grateful for it.

He found it under his NASA shuttle paperweight and handed it to her.

"It isn't terrible, just not up to your usual standard," he said handing her a paper marked B minus.

Maddy stared at the page. Her eyes filled with tears as she fumbled in her folder looking for the sheet of paper she had placed there earlier.

Mr. Daniels took her tears in stride. "It's not the end of the world, my little over-achiever," he said kindly, "Why don't we go over it together?"

Maddy shook her head. "It's not the grade; I knew it wasn't very good," she was barely able to form the words.

She handed him the page she had taken from her folder. Mr. Daniels took it with a puzzled look. After a moment he began to look it over quietly. Then he read:

In Our House

In our house

We all pretend

That all is well,

No one offends.
We do our jobs,
We go to school,
To church, to work,
They all are fooled.
The surface of our lives seems clear,
The mark of shame does not appear,
It's hidden far beneath the shell,
And those who know must never tell.
In our house
We all pretend
That all is well,
No one offends.
Our lessons learned,
Our counsel kept,
Our minds stay silent,
Our souls have wept.
The pain asleep though always there,
We mustn't let it linger where,
It festers with time until grown,
Into a cancer of its own.
So, in your house,
Do not pretend
That all is well
If one offends.

———————◉———————

WHEN HE FINISHED HE was thoughtful. After a few moments he took out a red pencil and graded it A+ before returning his attention to his student.

"You're ready to stop pretending, aren't you?" he asked.

Maddy nodded, she wanted to say something, but words failed to come.

"Maybe I can help you do this," suggested Mr. Daniels, "Why don't we go find Mrs. Lunsford together?"

Alex's Essay

———————●———————

I VISITED MY GRANDMOTHER at Whispering Pines last week. She has lived there for almost a year now and I try to visit every other weekend. It's close to our house and I can ride my bike there. I told her about school and she listened with interest, complimenting my achievements and reminding me about how important it is to always do my best. Of course, during much of the visit she didn't know who I was, but seemed happy to have company.

Nana hasn't always been like this. I remember baking cookies and reading stories together when I was little, all the typical grandmother-grandchild activities. She also enjoyed doing things not so typically associated with grandmothers, like riding roller coasters and parasailing. She even took flying lessons for a while although she never got her pilot's license. Grandpa used to call her Nana Knievel back then.

When I was seven years old, I noticed that her left hand would shake when she held the book we were reading together. That's when I became the "official book holder". Then we learned that she has Parkinson's disease which mostly affects movement. It's not a disease that you can catch, but doctors don't know what causes it. The good news is that it does not affect speech or intelligence. The bad news is that it is what they call a progressive disease so it gets worse over time.

Nana has always had a good attitude about her illness. She used to say, "We'll just have to work around it." She had to give up flying lessons and roller coasters and said she was glad she did those things while she could.

When I was ten years old, I overheard my mother and uncle worrying about Nana's forgetfulness. I had noticed it myself when Nana stopped in the middle of telling a story trying to remember a name. Nana would just laugh and call it a "senior moment". My uncle seemed to think things were getting worse. Now Nana was forgetting the names of common objects like forks and combs. My mother didn't believe him at first, but she agreed to stop in and check on Nana and Grandpa more often.

Unfortunately, my uncle was right to worry. The doctors never officially called it Alzheimer's Disease but that's what our family calls it. I have done some reading and I learned that memory loss and slow thinking are also symptoms of Parkinson's Disease. Sometimes I think I might like to become a researcher or doctor to learn all I can about neurological diseases.

Meanwhile, I still enjoy visiting Nana when I can. I made her a scrapbook with photographs of people she knows and their names. She looks at it sometimes to help her remember. We still like to read together only now I do all the reading.

During our visit last week Nana listened quietly as I read Edgar Allan Poe's "The Tell-Tale Heart" which seemed a good choice since Halloween had just passed. When I finished reading she said, "Alex, never pass up the chance to experience all that life has to offer." I was surprised to hear her call me by name because she seldom does anymore, I looked up and replied assuring her that I would, but she only stared vacantly out the window and then turned to me with a slightly confused expression. I allowed myself a moment to feel sad, but knowing that Nana herself would simply "buck up" and "work around it" I closed the book, gave her a kiss, and told her I would come again for another visit soon.

Michael's Essay

———◉———

I HAVE OFTEN HEARD my mother tell people that she "does not work outside the home". She is such a liar. She works all the time: inside the home, outside the home, you name it. What she means is she doesn't get paid for the work she does.

Volunteer work is still work and my mother does a lot of volunteering. For example, my mother belongs to Women's Club. What do its members do? They conduct charity fundraisers for scholarships and other deserving causes. Since she is the club treasurer she works hard keeping tract of funds raised and making sure they reach their target beneficiaries.

My school is lucky to have her volunteer in the library once a week. She not only doesn't get paid, but often ends up *spending* money on things she decides the school should have. Sometimes it's something small like materials for a bulletin board display. At other times she will donate an item like a new printer for the librarian who was using an old dot matrix model that used reams of pin-fed paper. (Good grief! Dot matrix? Pin-fed paper? Is this the Stone Age?) For really big projects she'll rally the parents at a PTA meeting and organize a fund raiser. It probably won't surprise you at this point to learn that she is the president of the Chase Middle School Parent Teacher Association.

My mother, however, is one of those parents who is always underfoot. I can't go anywhere without her (of course, I can't drive yet so that's part of the problem!) She's always around reminding me, nagging me, and generally making sure I'm taking care of things. Since she's so involved at school, she is able to pop in on me once in a while often bringing me things she thinks I've forgotten. I have to tell you this is *not* cool in middle school.

We recently had a conversation about this. To be perfectly honest she had found a list of grievances I had drawn up outlining my complaints and – there really should be dramatic music at this point – *I caught her reading it in my room!* It was an awkward moment for both of us. I apologized for writing it, she apologized for reading it and then we talked.

It was a good talk. I declared my independence explaining that I wanted to manage the responsibilities of middle school on my own, mistakes included. Mom agreed to work on it and, so far, she has been true to her word. When I told one of my friends about our conversation, she couldn't get over the fact that my mother didn't yell at me or punish me at all. When I told her my mother had *apologized* she was amazed.

Come to think of it I guess I did get pretty lucky when God was passing out mothers (Dad, you're not so bad either, but right now the subject is Mom). True, she sometimes seems to follow me like a stalker, but I guess there are far worse things than having a mother who cares and takes the time to show it.

Maddy's Essay

———————●———————

I HAVE A FIVE-YEAR-old sister named Cassie. Her full name is Mary Cassidy Schmidt, but she goes by Cassie. The Cassidy comes from my grandmother's maiden name on my father's side of the family. She would definitely want you to know this information, if you knew her, you'd know what I mean. She has very definite opinions about things. That's one of the things I like about her so much.

Yep, that's right: I like her. Some people are surprised to find out that I enjoy spending time with a five-year-old kid, but I do. She talks a lot, she always wants to be included, and she never lets you forget she's around.

Cassie has lots of characteristics that I admire. She's enthusiastic, curious and patient. I suppose most kids are enthusiastic and curious, but how many truly patient five-year-olds are there? For example, last week I watched her attempt to eat spaghetti by spinning it on a fork. She spun and dropped spaghetti back onto her plate for more than half an hour, but only a few of the slippery strands ever made it to her mouth. Did she get upset? Nope, not even a little. Did she give up in frustration? No, although she did eventually decide that the main course was over and move on to dessert. Did she feel terrible about her failure? I doubt it by the way she smiled over her vanilla ice cream. I remember thinking at the time that I wished I could be more like her instead of worrying over every little mistake, or not trying something new because I might not be good at it right away.

Once in a while I am asked to look after Cassie while my parents are out. Of course, this includes things like making sure she doesn't watch too much TV, eats a good dinner, has her bath and gets to bed on time. When we go out I am often asked to watch out for her so I take her hand while we cross the street, insist she stay with me when we are shopping, and warn her against talking to strangers. I take these responsibilities very seriously.

I worry sometimes about more than her safety. I worry about how she will feel when she discovers one day that the world is not always a friendly place, that sometimes people will make fun of your failures or even enjoy them. Will she lose her enthusiasm when that happens? Will her patience be exhausted when she learns that life is sometimes a race to be the first to complete a task? Will her curiosity be less when she finds out more than she really wants to know about something or someone?

Cassie is smart. She quickly learned the ropes at school: be in your seat when the bell rings, don't cut in line, and raise your hand to speak. I'm sure she'll be able to take care of herself and I know I can't always be there to watch over her. I just want her to know that I will always protect her if I can; that she can count on me to do what might need to be done. Sometimes people you trust let you down; I just don't want her to learn that lesson from me.

Author's Note

———————●●———————

AS MR. KNOWLES TELLS the students: "write what you know". I have attempted to do just that. I have spent many years in libraries and classrooms so I am comfortable writing about this setting.

I am also familiar with the problem Maddy faces with her father. I only mention this to say that it is a problem that can be overcome. It is possible to be successful and happy in life even with this very difficult beginning.

Maddy's problem is one that is rarely discussed which benefits the abuser. Children who suffer this type of abuse somehow know that it is a secret thing. The abuser is usually someone in a position of authority, and often someone who should be providing safety and security. All of these factors make it very hard for the abused to find a voice.

This book is my attempt to bring awareness and discussion to this topic. In a world with commercials for whole body deodorant, incontinence, and other once unmentionable topics, it's time we made room for a discussion about this type of sexual abuse. The more it comes into the open, the harder it will be for the abuser to succeed.

Acknowledgements

I WOULD LIKE TO THANK my usual group of readers who help me find all the errors my own eyes refuse to see. Alieda Maron, many thanks for your proofreading and encouragement. I really think this book may have rested comfortably in my computer document file without your gentle, but insistent push. Thanks also to Tina Neville, another friend who has taught me, among other things, to look for the positive. Even your criticisms come couched in an eye that attempts to see things from every angle. Lynn Wilson, who may not recognize her contribution, also deserves my thanks as someone who saw me through some of the hardest of times.

I cannot forget to thank my husband, who could give lessons on being the kind of father every child deserves. He also serves as proofreader and able navigator of publishing platforms. Thanks for your dog-with-a-bone persistence!

And to my big sister for so many reasons. Many thanks for being the mother to me that you didn't have for yourself. Not sure who your role model was to fashion you into the truly marvelous woman you have become, but I was lucky to have you as an example. This book was for you.

About the Author

S.L. Sumner is a former librarian who has worked in schools and libraries. When she isn't writing she likes to curl up with one or both of her delightful terriers and a good book.

In 8th grade her English teacher had the class keep a journal for a grading period. When it was returned the teacher wrote: "When you're a writer I'll collect your books." She never forgot those words and hopes that the reader will enjoy her efforts as much as Mrs. DePaula once did.